PENGUIN POPULAR CLASSICS

ANTONY AND CLEOPATRA
BY WILLIAM SHAKESPEARE

PENGUIN POPULAR CLASSICS

ANTONY AND CLEOPATRA

WILLIAM SHAKESPEARE

PENGUIN BOOKS

PENGUIN BOOKS

Published by the Penguin Group
Penguin Books Ltd, 27 Wrights Lane, London w8 5tz, England
Penguin Putnam Inc., 375 Hudson Street, New York, New York 10014, USA
Penguin Books Australia Ltd, Ringwood, Victoria, Australia
Penguin Books Canada Ltd, 10 Alcorn Avenue, Toronto, Ontario, Canada m4v 3b2
Penguin Books (NZ) Ltd, Private Bag 102902, NSMC, Auckland, New Zealand

Penguin Books Ltd, Registered Offices: Harmondsworth, Middlesex, England

Published in Penguin Popular Classics 1994
9

Copyright 1938 by the Estate of G. B. Harrison

Printed in Great Britain by Cox & Wyman Ltd, Reading, Berkshire

CONTENTS

*

THE WORKS OF SHAKESPEARE

PLAYS

APPROXIMATE DATE			FIRST PRINTED
Before 1594	HENRY VI *three parts*	*Folio*	1623
	RICHARD III		1597
	TITUS ANDRONICUS		1594
	LOVE'S LABOUR'S LOST		1598
	THE TWO GENTLEMEN OF VERONA		*Folio*
	THE COMEDY OF ERRORS		*Folio*
	THE TAMING OF THE SHREW		*Folio*
1594–1597	ROMEO AND JULIET (*pirated* 1597)		1599
	A MIDSUMMER NIGHT'S DREAM		1600
	RICHARD II		1597
	KING JOHN		*Folio*
	THE MERCHANT OF VENICE		1600
1597–1600	HENRY IV *part i*		1598
	HENRY IV *part ii*		1600
	HENRY V (*pirated* 1600)		*Folio*
	MUCH ADO ABOUT NOTHING		1600
	MERRY WIVES OF WINDSOR (*pirated* 1602)		*Folio*
	AS YOU LIKE IT		*Folio*
	JULIUS CAESAR		*Folio*
	TROYLUS AND CRESSIDA		1609
1601–1608	HAMLET (*pirated* 1603)		1604
	TWELFTH NIGHT		*Folio*
	MEASURE FOR MEASURE		*Folio*
	ALL'S WELL THAT ENDS WELL		*Folio*
	OTHELLO		1622
	LEAR		1608
	MACBETH		*Folio*
	TIMON OF ATHENS		*Folio*
	ANTONY AND CLEOPATRA		*Folio*
	CORIOLANUS		*Folio*
After 1608	PERICLES (*omitted from the Folio*)		1609
	CYMBELINE		*Folio*
	THE WINTER'S TALE		*Folio*
	THE TEMPEST		*Folio*
	HENRY VIII		*Folio*

POEMS

DATES UNKNOWN		
	VENUS AND ADONIS	1593
	THE RAPE OF LUCRECE	1594
	SONNETS } A LOVER'S COMPLAINT }	1609
	THE PHOENIX AND THE TURTLE	1601

WILLIAM SHAKESPEARE

William Shakespeare was born at Stratford upon Avon in April, 1564. He was the third child, and eldest son, of John Shakespeare and Mary Arden. His father was one of the most prosperous men of Stratford, who held in turn the chief offices in the town. His mother was of gentle birth, the daughter of Robert Arden of Wilmcote. In December, 1582, Shakespeare married Ann Hathaway, daughter of a farmer of Shottery, near Stratford; their first child Susanna was baptized on May 6, 1583, and twins, Hamnet and Judith, on February 22, 1585. Little is known of Shakespeare's early life; but it is unlikely that a writer who dramatized such an incomparable range and variety of human kinds and experiences should have spent his early manhood entirely in placid pursuits in a country town. There is one tradition, not universally accepted, that he fled from Stratford because he was in trouble for deer stealing, and had fallen foul of Sir Thomas Lucy, the local magnate; another that he was for some time a schoolmaster.

From 1592 onwards the records are much fuller. In March, 1592, the Lord Strange's players produced a new play at the Rose Theatre called *Harry the Sixth*, which was very successful, and was probably the *First Part of Henry VI*. In the autumn of 1592 Robert Greene, the best known of the professional writers, as he was dying wrote a letter to three fellow writers in which he warned them against the ingratitude of players in general, and in particular against an 'upstart crow' who 'supposes he is as much able to bombast out a blank verse as the best of you: and being an absolute Johannes Factotum is in his own conceit the only

Shake-scene in a country.' This is the first reference to Shakespeare, and the whole passage suggests that Shakespeare had become suddenly famous as a playwright. At this time Shakespeare was brought into touch with Edward Alleyne the great tragedian, and Christopher Marlowe, whose thundering parts of Tamburlaine, the Jew of Malta, and Dr Faustus Alleyne was acting, as well as Hieronimo, the hero of Kyd's *Spanish Tragedy*, the most famous of all Elizabethan plays.

In April, 1593, Shakespeare published his poem *Venus and Adonis*, which was dedicated to the young Earl of Southampton: it was a great and lasting success, and was reprinted nine times in the next few years. In May, 1594, his second poem, *The Rape of Lucrece*, was also dedicated to Southampton.

There was little playing in 1593, for the theatres were shut during a severe outbreak of the plague; but in the autumn of 1594, when the plague ceased, the playing companies were reorganized, and Shakespeare became a sharer in the Lord Chamberlain's company who went to play in the Theatre in Shoreditch. During these months Marlowe and Kyd had died. Shakespeare was thus for a time without a rival. He had already written the three parts of *Henry VI*, *Richard III*, *Titus Andronicus*, *The Two Gentlemen of Verona*, *Love's Labour's Lost*, *The Comedy of Errors*, and *The Taming of the Shrew*. Soon afterwards he wrote the first of his greater plays – *Romeo and Juliet* – and he followed this success in the next three years with *A Midsummer Night's Dream*, *Richard II*, and *The Merchant of Venice*. The two parts of *Henry IV*, introducing Falstaff, the most popular of all his comic characters, were written in 1597-8.

The company left the Theatre in 1597 owing to disputes over a renewal of the ground lease, and went to play at the

Curtain in the same neighbourhood. The disputes contin-
ued throughout 1598, and at Christmas the players settled
the matter by demolishing the old Theatre and re-erecting
a new playhouse on the South bank of the Thames, near
Southwark Cathedral. This playhouse was named the
Globe. The expenses of the new building were shared by
the chief members of the Company, including Shakespeare,
who was now a man of some means. In 1596 he had bought
New Place, a large house in the centre of Stratford, for £60,
and through his father purchased a coat-of-arms from the
Heralds, which was the official recognition that he and his
family were gentlefolk.

By the summer of 1598 Shakespeare was recognized as
the greatest of English dramatists. Booksellers were print-
ing his more popular plays, at times even in pirated or stolen
versions, and he received a remarkable tribute from a young
writer named Francis Meres, in his book *Palladis Tamia*. In
a long catalogue of English authors Meres gave Shakespeare
more prominence than any other writer, and mentioned by
name twelve of his plays.

Shortly before the Globe was opened, Shakespeare had
completed the cycle of plays dealing with the whole story
of the Wars of the Roses with *Henry V*. It was followed by
As You Like it, and *Julius Caesar*, the first of the maturer
tragedies. In the next three years he wrote *Troilus and
Cressida*, *The Merry Wives of Windsor*, *Hamlet*, and *Twelfth
Night*.

On March 24, 1603, Queen Elizabeth died. The company
had often performed before her, but they found her suc-
cessor a far more enthusiastic patron. One of the first acts
of King James was to take over the company and to promote them to be his own servants, so that henceforward
they were known as the King's Men. They acted now very

frequently at Court, and prospered accordingly. In the early years of the reign Shakespeare wrote the more sombre comedies, *All's Well that Ends Well*, and *Measure for Measure*, which were followed by *Othello*, *Macbeth*, and *King Lear*. Then he returned to Roman themes with *Antony and Cleopatra* and *Coriolanus*.

Since 1601 Shakespeare had been writing less, and there were now a number of rival dramatists who were introducing new styles of drama, particularly Ben Jonson (whose first successful comedy, *Every Man in his Humour*, was acted by Shakespeare's company in 1598), Chapman, Dekker, Marston, and Beaumont and Fletcher who began to write in 1607. In 1608 the King's Men acquired a second playhouse, an indoor private theatre in the fashionable quarter of the Blackfriars. At private theatres, plays were performed indoors; the prices charged were higher than in the public playhouses, and the audience consequently was more select. Shakespeare seems to have retired from the stage about this time: his name does not occur in the various lists of players after 1607. Henceforward he lived for the most part at Stratford, where he was regarded as one of the most important citizens. He still wrote a few plays, and he tried his hand at the new form of tragi-comedy – a play with tragic incidents but a happy ending – which Beaumont and Fletcher had popularized. He wrote four of these – *Pericles*, *Cymbeline*, *The Winter's Tale*, and *The Tempest*, which was acted at Court in 1611. For the last four years of his life he lived in retirement. His son Hamnet had died in 1596: his two daughters were now married. Shakespeare died at Stratford upon Avon on April 23, 1616, and was buried in the chancel of the church, before the high altar. Shortly afterwards a memorial which still exists, with a portrait bust, was set up on the North wall. His wife survived him.

When Shakespeare died fourteen of his plays had been separately published in Quarto booklets. In 1623 his surviving fellow actors, John Heming and Henry Condell, with the co-operation of a number of printers, published a collected edition of thirty-six plays in one Folio volume, with an engraved portrait, memorial verses by Ben Jonson and others, and an Epistle to the Reader in which Heming and Condell make the interesting note that Shakespeare's 'hand and mind went together, and what he thought, he uttered with that easiness that we have scarce received from him a blot in his papers.'

The plays as printed in the Quartos or the Folio differ considerably from the usual modern text. They are often not divided into scenes, and sometimes not even into acts. Nor are there place-headings at the beginning of each scene, because in the Elizabethan theatre there was no scenery. They are carelessly printed and the spelling is erratic.

THE ELIZABETHAN THEATRE

Although plays of one sort and another had been acted for many generations, no permanent playhouse was erected in England until 1576. In the 1570's the Lord Mayor and Aldermen of the City of London and the players were constantly at variance. As a result James Burbage, then the leader of the great Earl of Leicester's players, decided that he would erect a playhouse outside the jurisdiction of the Lord Mayor, where the players would no longer be hindered by the authorities. Accordingly in 1576 he built the Theatre in Shoreditch, at that time a suburb of London. The experiment was successful, and by 1592 there were two more playhouses in London, the Curtain (also in Shore-ditch), and the Rose on the south bank of the river, near Southwark Cathedral.

Elizabethan players were accustomed to act on a variety of stages; in the great hall of a nobleman's house, or one of the Queen's palaces, in town halls and in yards, as well as their own theatre.

The public playhouse for which most of Shakespeare's plays were written was a small and intimate affair. The outside measurement of the Fortune Theatre, which was built in 1600 to rival the new Globe, was but eighty feet square. Playhouses were usually circular or hexagonal, with three tiers of galleries looking down upon the yard or pit, which was open to the sky. The stage jutted out into the yard so that the actors came forward into the midst of their audience.

Over the stage there was a roof, and on either side doors by which the characters entered or disappeared. Over the back of the stage ran a gallery or upper stage which was used whenever an upper scene was needed, as when Romeo climbs up to Juliet's bedroom, or the citizens of Angiers address King John from the walls. The space beneath this upper stage was known as the tiring house; it was concealed from the audience by a curtain which could be drawn back to reveal an inner stage, for such scenes as the witches' cave in Macbeth, Prospero's cell, or Juliet's tomb.

There was no general curtain concealing the whole stage, so that all scenes on the main stage began with an entrance and ended with an exit. Thus in tragedies the dead must be carried away. There was no scenery, and therefore no limit to the number of scenes, for a scene came to an end when the characters left the stage. When it was necessary for the exact locality of a scene to be known, then Shakespeare

THE GLOBE THEATRE

Wood-engraving by R. J. Beedham after a reconstruction by J. C. Adams

indicated it in the dialogue; otherwise a simple property or a garment was sufficient; a chair or stool showed an indoor scene, a man wearing riding boots was a messenger, a king wearing armour was on the battlefield, or the like. Such simplicity was on the whole an advantage; the spectator was not distracted by the setting and Shakespeare was able to use as many scenes as he wished. The action passed by very quickly: a play of 2500 lines of verse could be acted in two hours. Moreover, since the actor was so close to his audience, the slightest subtlety of voice and gesture was easily appreciated.

The company was a 'Fellowship of Players', who were all partners and sharers. There were usually ten to fifteen full members, with three or four boys, and some paid servants. Shakespeare had therefore to write for his team. The chief actor in the company was Richard Burbage, who first distinguished himself as Richard III; for him Shakespeare wrote his great tragic parts. An important member of the company was the clown or low comedian. From 1594 to 1600 the company's clown was Will Kemp; he was succeeded by Robert Armin. No women were allowed to appear on the stage, and all women's parts were taken by boys.

ANTONY AND CLEOPATRA

The Tragedy of Antony and Cleopatra was apparently written in 1606 or 1607. On 20th May 1608 the Stationers' Register records the entry of two plays to Edward Blount, the stationer, the first being 'A book called The book of Pericles Prince of Tyre', and the second 'A book called Antony and Cleopatra'. *Pericles* was published in a Quarto in 1609, but *Antony and Cleopatra* was not printed separately and appeared first in the Folio of 1623. The play may have been a year or more old when it was entered, for in 1607 Samuel Daniel, who had already published a tragedy called *Cleopatra* written in the Senecan manner in 1594, brought out a new edition with alterations that resemble passages in Shakespeare's play. *Antony and Cleopatra* thus followed *Macbeth* and *Lear*.

Antony and Cleopatra is the sequel to Shakespeare's *Julius Cæsar*, written about 1599. Shakespeare took the story of the play from Plutarch's *Life of Marcus Antonius*. Plutarch was a Greek who died about A.D. 120. He wrote a series of parallel lives of Greeks and Romans, and being less interested in history than in personality, he recorded vivid anecdotes and sayings which reveal character. These *Lives* were translated into French by Jacques Amyot, and from the French into English by Sir Thomas North in 1579. A second edition of North's Plutarch appeared in 1595. In writing *Julius Cæsar* Shakespeare had vastly simplified history by selecting suitable passages from the Lives of Julius Cæsar, Marcus Brutus, and Marcus Antonius. There was far less difficulty in the story of Antony and Cleopatra, and he followed Plutarch's Life of Antony closely, at times

even translating North's prose into blank verse. Enobarbus'
account of Antony's first meeting with Cleopatra p. 51,
l. 19, one of the finest pieces of descriptive writing in all
Shakespeare, appeared in North's translation thus:

'Therefore, when she was sent unto by divers letters,
both from Antonius himself and also from his friends, she
made so light of it, and mocked Antonius so much, that
she disdained to set forward otherwise, but to take her barge
in the river of Cydnus; the poop whereof was of gold, the
sails of purple, and the oars of silver, which kept stroke in
rowing after the sound of the music of flutes, howboys,
cithernes, viols and such other instruments as they played
upon in the barge. And now for the person of her self,
she was laid under a pavilion of cloth of gold of tissue,
apparelled and attired like the goddess Venus, commonly
drawn in picture: and hard by her, on either hand of her,
pretty fair boys apparelled as painters do set forth god
Cupid, with little fans in their hands, with the which they
fanned wind upon her. Her ladies and gentlewomen also
the fairest of them, were apparelled like the nymphs
Nereids (which are the mermaids of the waters) and like
the Graces; some steering the helm, others tending the
tackle and ropes of the barge, out of the which there came
a wonderful passing sweet savour of perfumes, that perfumed the wharf's side, pestered with innumerable multitudes of people. Some of them followed the barge all along
the river-side: others also ran out of the city to see her
coming in. So that in the end, there ran such multitudes of
people one after another to see her, that Antonius was left
post alone in the market-place, in his imperial seat, to give
audience: and there went a rumour in the people's mouths,
that the goddess Venus was come to play with the god
Bacchus, for the general good of all Asia. When Cleopatra

landed, Antonius sent to invite her to supper to him. But she sent him word again, he should do better rather to come and sup with her. Antonius therefore, to show himself courteous unto her at her arrival, was contented to obey her, and went to supper to her: where he found such passing sumptuous fare, that no tongue can express it.'

Plutarch's account of the death of Cleopatra, dramatized on p. 137, l. 11, is that Cleopatra first lamented over Antony's tomb, then 'having ended these doleful plaints, and crowned the tomb with garlands and sundry nosegays, and marvellous lovingly embraced the same, she commanded they should prepare her bath: and when she had bathed and washed herself, she fell to her meat, and was sumptuously served. Now whilst she was at dinner, there came a countryman and brought her a basket. The soldiers that warded at the gates, asked him straight what he had in his basket. He opened his basket, and took out the leaves that covered the figs, and shewed them that they were figs he brought. They all of them marvelled to see so goodly figs. The countryman laughed to hear them, and bade them take some if they would. They believed he told them truly and so bade him carry them in. After Cleopatra had dined, she sent a certain table written and sealed unto Cæsar, and commanded them all to go out of the tombs where she was, but the two women; then she shut the doors to her. Cæsar, when he had received this table, and began to read her lamentation and petition, requesting him that he would let her be buried with Antonius, found straight what she meant, and thought to have gone either himself: howbeit, he sent one before in all haste that might be, to see what it was. Her death was very sudden; for those whom Cæsar sent unto her ran thither in all haste possible, and found the soldiers standing at the gate, mistrusting nothing, nor understanding of her death. But when they had opened the doors, they found Cleopatra stark-dead, laid upon a bed of gold, attired and arrayed in her royal robes, and one of her two women, which was called Iras, dead at her feet: and her other woman (called Charmian) half dead, and trembling, trimming the diadem which Cleopatra wore upon her head. One of the soldiers seeing her, angrily said unto her: "Is that well done, Charmian?" "Very well," said she again, "and meet for a princess descended from the race of so many noble kings": she said no more, but fell down dead hard by the bed.'

Antony and Cleopatra was first printed in the First Folio of 1623. It is not an easy text, for although there are not many errors or misprints, there are a number of passages which cause difficulty. The play was written when Shakespeare's style was most intense, and his poetic imagery peculiarly pregnant and concentrated; some of the difficulties are due to this excessive compression of thought. The punctuation (with occasional lapses) is, after the Elizabethan custom, dramatic and sensitive. The verse at times is very free, particularly at the beginning and ending of speeches, and it is clear that many of the verse lines (as in *Macbeth*) were not written in the formal five-stress metre. There is no division into Acts and Scenes in the Folio; nor in the play are there any natural breaks in the action, which is rapid and continuous.

As a result Shakespeare's editors have havocked *Antony and Cleopatra* more drastically than usual. They have generously emended the text, supplied names from Plutarch where Shakespeare omitted them or set him right where he gave another name to a character, invented stage business impossible on the Elizabethan stage, reduced the punctuation (at times completely altering the sense) to modern convention, rearranged the verse lines, and divided the play into five Acts and forty-two scenes.

The present text follows the Folio more closely. Spelling has been modernized, but the original arrangement and punctuation (which shows how the speeches should be delivered) have been kept except where they seemed definitely wrong. Only a few of the many emendations have been kept. The reader who is used to the 'accepted text' will thus find certain unfamiliarities, but the text itself is nearer to that used in Shakespeare's own playhouse.

The Tragedy of
Antony and Cleopatra

THE ACTORS' NAMES

ANTONY
OCTAVIUS CÆSAR } triumvirs
LEPIDUS
SEXTUS POMPEIUS
DOMITIUS ENOBARBUS
VENTIDIUS
EROS
SCARUS } friends to Antony
DERCETAS
DEMETRIUS
PHILO
MÆCENAS
AGRIPPA
DOLABELLA
PROCULEIUS } friends to Cæsar
THIDIAS
GALLUS
MENAS
MENECRATES } friends to Sextus Pompeius
VARRIUS
TAURUS, general to Cæsar
CANIDIUS, general to Antony
SILIUS, an officer in Ventidius's army
An ambassador from Antony to Cæsar
ALEXAS
MARDIAN, a eunuch
RANNIUS
LUCILIUS } attendants on Cleopatra
SELEUCUS
DIOMEDES
LAMPRIUS, a Soothsayer
A Clown

CLEOPATRA, queen of Egypt
OCTAVIA, sister to Cæsar, and wife to Antony
CHARMIAN } attendants on Cleopatra
IRAS
Officers, Soldiers, Messengers, Attendants

I. 1

Enter Demetrius and Philo.

PHILO: Nay, but this dotage of our General's
O'erflows the measure: those his goodly eyes
That o'er the files and musters of the war,
Have glow'd like plated Mars,
Now bend, now turn
The office and devotion of their view
Upon a tawny front. His Captain's heart,
Which in the scuffles of great fights hath burst
The buckles on his breast, reneges all temper,
And is become the bellows and the fan
To cool a gipsy's lust.

*Flourish. Enter Antony, Cleopatra, her Ladies, the train,
with Eunuchs fanning her.*

Look where they come:
Take but good note, and you shall see in him
(The triple pillar of the world) transform'd
Into a strumpet's fool. Behold and see.

CLEOPATRA: If it be love indeed, tell me how much.

ANTONY: There's beggary in the love that can be reckon'd.

CLEOPATRA: I'll set a bourn how far to be belov'd.

ANTONY: Then must thou needs find out new Heaven,
new Earth.

Enter a Messenger.

MESSENGER: News (my good Lord) from Rome.

ANTONY: Grates me, the sum.

CLEOPATRA: Nay hear them Antony.
Fulvia perchance is angry: or who knows,
If the scarce-bearded Cæsar have not sent

His powerful mandate to you. Do this, or this;
Take in that Kingdom, and enfranchise that:
Perform 't, or else we damn thee.

ANTONY: How, my Love?

CLEOPATRA: Perchance? Nay, and most like:
You must not stay here longer, your dismission
Is come from Cæsar, therefore hear it Antony.
Where's Fulvia's process? (Cæsar's I would say)
    both?
Call in the messengers: as I am Egypt's Queen,
Thou blushest Antony, and that blood of thine
Is Cæsar's homager: else so thy cheek pays shame,
When shrill-tongu'd Fulvia scolds. The messengers.

ANTONY: Let Rome in Tiber melt, and the wide arch
Of the rang'd Empire fall: here is my space,
Kingdoms are clay: our dungy earth alike
Feeds beast as man; the nobleness of life
Is to do thus: when such a mutual pair,
And such a twain can do't, in which I bind
On pain of punishment, the world to weet
We stand up peerless.

CLEOPATRA: Excellent falsehood:
Why did he marry Fulvia, and not love her?
I'll seem the fool I am not. Antony will be himself.

ANTONY: But stirr'd by Cleopatra.
Now for the love of Love, and her soft hours,
Let's not confound the time with conference harsh;
There's not a minute of our lives should stretch
Without some pleasure now. What sport to-night?

CLEOPATRA: Hear the Ambassadors.

ANTONY: Fie wrangling Queen:
Whom every thing becomes, to chide, to laugh,
To weep: whose every passion fully strives

To make itself (in thee) fair, and admir'd.
No messenger but thine, and all alone, to-night
We'll wander through the streets, and note
The qualities of people. Come my Queen,
Last night you did desire it. Speak not to us.
                    Exeunt with the train.
DEMETRIUS: Is Cæsar with Antonius priz'd so slight?
PHILO: Sir sometimes when he is not Antony,
He comes too short of that great property
Which still should go with Antony.
DEMETRIUS: I am full sorry, that he approves the common
liar who thus speaks of him at Rome; but I will hope of
better deeds to-morrow. Rest you happy.
                    Exeunt.

I. 2

Enter Enobarbus, Lamprius, a Soothsayer, Rannius, Lucilius,
Charmian, Iras, Mardian the Eunuch, and Alexas.

CHARMIAN: Lord Alexas, sweet Alexas, most any thing
Alexas, almost most absolute Alexas, where's the Sooth-
sayer that you prais'd so to th' Queen? Oh that I knew
this husband, which you say, must change his horns with
garlands.
ALEXAS: Soothsayer.
SOOTHSAYER: Your will?
CHARMIAN: Is this the man? Is't you sir that know things?
SOOTHSAYER: In Nature's infinite book of secrecy, a little
I can read.
ALEXAS: Show him your hand.
ENOBARBUS: Bring in the banquet quickly: wine enough,
Cleopatra's health to drink.
CHARMIAN: Good sir, give me good fortune.

SOOTHSAYER: I make not, but foresee.

CHARMIAN: Pray then, foresee me one.

SOOTHSAYER: You shall be yet far fairer than you are.

CHARMIAN: He means in flesh.

IRAS: No, you shall paint when you are old.

CHARMIAN: Wrinkles forbid.

ALEXAS: Vex not his prescience, be attentive.

CHARMIAN: Hush.

SOOTHSAYER: You shall be more beloving, than beloved.

CHARMIAN: I had rather heat my liver with drinking.

ALEXAS: Nay, hear him.

CHARMIAN: Good now some excellent fortune: let me be married to three Kings in a forenoon, and widow them all: let me have a child at fifty, to whom Herod of Jewry may do homage. Find me to marry me with Octavius Cæsar, and companion me with my Mistress.

SOOTHSAYER: You shall outlive the Lady whom you serve.

CHARMIAN: Oh excellent, I love long life better than figs.

SOOTHSAYER: You have seen and proved a fairer former fortune, than that which is to approach.

CHARMIAN: Then belike my children shall have no names: prithee how many boys and wenches must I have?

SOOTHSAYER: If every of your wishes had a womb, and fertile every wish, a million.

CHARMIAN: Out fool, I forgive thee for a witch.

ALEXAS: You think none but your sheets are privy to your wishes.

CHARMIAN: Nay come, tell Iras hers.

ALEXAS: We'll know all our fortunes.

ENOBARBUS: Mine, and most of our fortunes to-night, shall be drunk to bed.

IRAS: There's a palm presages chastity, if nothing else.

CHARMIAN: E'en as the o'erflowing Nilus presageth famine.

IRAS: Go you wild bedfellow, you cannot soothsay.

CHARMIAN: Nay, if an oily palm be not a fruitful prognostication, I cannot scratch mine ear. Prithee tell her but a worky day fortune.

SOOTHSAYER: Your fortunes are alike.

IRAS: But how, but how, give me particulars.

SOOTHSAYER: I have said.

IRAS: Am I not an inch of fortune better than she?

CHARMIAN: Well, if you were but an inch of fortune better than I, where would you choose it?

IRAS: Not in my husband's nose.

CHARMIAN: Our worser thoughts Heavens mend.

ALEXAS: Come, his fortune, his fortune. Oh let him marry a woman that cannot go, sweet Isis, I beseech thee, and let her die too, and give him a worse, and let worse follow worse, till the worst of all follow him laughing to his grave, fifty-fold a cuckold. Good Isis hear me this prayer, though thou deny me a matter of more weight: good Isis I beseech thee.

IRAS: Amen, dear Goddess, hear that prayer of the people. For, as it is a heart-breaking to see a handsome man loose-wiv'd, so it is a deadly sorrow, to behold a foul knave uncuckolded: therefore dear Isis keep decorum, and fortune him accordingly.

CHARMIAN: Amen.

ALEXAS: Lo now, if it lay in their hands to make me a cuckold, they would make themselves whores, but they 'ld do 't.

Enter Cleopatra.

ENOBARBUS: Hush, here comes Antony.

CHARMIAN: Not he, the Queen.

CLEOPATRA: Saw you, my Lord?
ENOBARBUS: No Lady.
CLEOPATRA: Was he not here?
CHARMIAN: No Madam.
CLEOPATRA: He was dispos'd to mirth, but on the sudden
A Roman thought hath struck him.
Enobarbus?
ENOBARBUS: Madam.
CLEOPATRA: Seek him, and bring him hither: where 's
Alexas?
ALEXAS: Here at your service.
My Lord approaches.

Enter Antony with a Messenger.

CLEOPATRA: We will not look upon him:
Go with us.
Exeunt.

MESSENGER: Fulvia thy wife,
First came into the field.
ANTONY: Against my brother Lucius?
MESSENGER: Ay: but soon that war had end,
And the time's state
Made friends of them, jointing their force 'gainst Cæsar,
Whose better issue in the war from Italy,
Upon the first encounter drave them.
ANTONY: Well, what worst?
MESSENGER: The nature of bad news infects the teller.
ANTONY: When it concerns the fool or coward: on.
Things that are past, are done, with me. 'Tis thus,
Who tells me true, though in his tale lie death,
I hear him as he flatter'd.
MESSENGER: Labienus (this is stiff news)
Hath with his Parthian force

Extended Asia; from Euphrates his conquering
Banner shook, from Syria to Lydia,
And to Ionia, whilst —

ANTONY: Antony thou wouldst say.

MESSENGER: Oh my Lord.

ANTONY: Speak to me home,
Mince not the general tongue, name
Cleopatra as she is call'd in Rome:
Rail thou in Fulvia's phrase, and taunt my faults
With such full license, as both Truth and Malice
Have power to utter. Oh then we bring forth weeds,
When our quick winds lie still, and our ills told us
Is as our earing: fare thee well awhile.

MESSENGER: At your noble pleasure.

Exit.

Enter another Messenger.

ANTONY: From Sicyon how the news? Speak there.

1 MESSENGER: The man from Sicyon,
Is there such an one?

2 MESSENGER: He stays upon your will.

ANTONY: Let him appear:
These strong Egyptian fetters I must break,
Or lose myself in dotage.

Enter another Messenger with a letter.

What are you?

3 MESSENGER: Fulvia thy wife is dead.

ANTONY: Where died she?

3 MESSENGER: In Sicyon, her length of sickness,
With what else more serious,
Importeth thee to know, this bears.

ANTONY: Forbear me.

Exeunt Messengers.

There 's a great spirit gone, thus did I desire it:

What our contempts doth often hurl from us,
We wish it ours again. The present pleasure,
By revolution low'ring, does become
The opposite of itself: she 's good being gone,
The hand could pluck her back, that shov'd her on.
I must from this enchanting Queen break off,
Ten thousand harms, more than the ills I know
My idleness doth hatch.

Enter Enobarbus.

How now Enobarbus.

ENOBARBUS: What's your pleasure, Sir?

ANTONY: I must with haste from hence.

ENOBARBUS: Why then we kill all our women. We see how mortal an unkindness is to them, if they suffer our departure death's the word.

ANTONY: I must be gone.

ENOBARBUS: Under a compelling occasion, let women die. It were pity to cast them away for nothing, though between them and a great cause, they should be esteemed nothing. Cleopatra catching but the least noise of this, dies instantly: I have seen her die twenty times upon far poorer moment: I do think there is mettle in death, which commits some loving act upon her, she hath such a celerity in dying.

ANTONY: She is cunning past man's thought.

ENOBARBUS: Alack Sir no, her passions are made of nothing but the finest part of pure Love. We cannot call her winds and waters, sighs and tears: they are greater storms and tempests than almanacs can report. This cannot be cunning in her; if it be, she makes a shower of rain as well as Jove.

ANTONY: Would I had never seen her.

ENOBARBUS: Oh sir, you had then left unseen a wonderful

piece of work, which not to have been blest withal, would have discredited your travel.

ANTONY: Fulvia is dead.

ENOBARBUS: Sir.

ANTONY: Fulvia is dead.

ENOBARBUS: Fulvia?

ANTONY: Dead.

ENOBARBUS: Why, sir, give the Gods a thankful sacrifice: when it pleaseth their deities to take the wife of a man from him, it shows to man the tailors of the earth: comforting therein, that when old robes are worn out, there are members to make new. If there were no more women but Fulvia, then had you indeed a cut, and the case to be lamented: this grief is crown'd with consolation, your old smock brings forth a new petticoat, and indeed the tears live in an onion, that should water this sorrow.

ANTONY: The business she hath broached in the State,
Cannot endure my absence.

ENOBARBUS: And the business you have broach'd here cannot be without you, especially that of Cleopatra's, which wholly depends on your abode.

ANTONY: No more light answers:
Let our officers
Have notice what we purpose. I shall break
The cause of our expedience to the Queen,
And get her leave to part. For not alone
The death of Fulvia, with more urgent touches
Do strongly speak to us: but the letters too
Of many our contriving friends in Rome,
Petition us at home. Sextus Pompeius
Hath given the dare to Cæsar, and commands
The Empire of the sea. Our slippery people,
Whose love is never link'd to the deserver,

Till his deserts are past, begin to throw
Pompey the Great, and all his dignities
Upon his son, who high in name and power,
Higher than both in blood and life, stands up
For the main soldier. Whose quality going on,
The sides o' th' world may danger. Much is breeding,
Which like the courser's hair, hath yet but life,
And not a serpent's poison. Say our pleasure,
To such whose place is under us, require
Our quick remove from hence.
ENOBARBUS: I shall do 't.
> *Exeunt.*

I. 3

Enter Cleopatra, Charmian, Alexas, and Iras.

CLEOPATRA: Where is he?
CHARMIAN: I did not see him since.
CLEOPATRA: See where he is,
Who's with him, what he does:
I did not send you. If you find him sad,
Say I am dancing: if in mirth, report
That I am sudden sick. Quick, and return.
> *Exit Alexas.*

CHARMIAN: Madam, methinks if you did love him dearly,
You do not hold the method, to enforce
The like from him.
CLEOPATRA: What should I do, I do not?
CHARMIAN: In each thing give him way, cross him in
nothing.
CLEOPATRA: Thou teachest like a fool: the way to lose him.
CHARMIAN: Tempt him not so too far. I wish forbear,
In time we hate that which we often fear.

Enter Antony.

But here comes Antony.

CLEOPATRA: I am sick, and sullen.

ANTONY: I am sorry to give breathing to my purpose.

CLEOPATRA: Help me away dear Charmian, I shall fall,
It cannot be thus long, the sides of Nature
Will not sustain it.

ANTONY: Now my dearest Queen.

CLEOPATRA: Pray you stand farther from me.

ANTONY: What's the matter?

CLEOPATRA: I know by that same eye there's some good
news.
What says the married woman you may go?
Would she had never given you leave to come.
Let her not say 'tis I that keep you here,
I have no power upon you: hers you are.

ANTONY: The Gods best know.

CLEOPATRA: Oh never was there Queen
So mightily betrayed: yet at the first
I saw the treasons planted.

ANTONY: Cleopatra.

CLEOPATRA: Why should I think you can be mine, and
true,
(Though you in swearing shake the throned Gods)
Who have been false to Fulvia?
Riotous madness,
To be entangled with those mouth-made vows,
Which break themselves in swearing.

ANTONY: Most sweet Queen.

CLEOPATRA: Nay pray you seek no colour for your going,
But bid farewell, and go:
When you sued staying,
Then was the time for words: no going then,

Eternity was in our lips, and eyes,
Bliss in our brows' bent: none our parts so poor,
But was a race of Heaven. They are so still,
Or thou the greatest soldier of the world,
Art turn'd the greatest liar.

ANTONY: How now Lady?

CLEOPATRA: I would I had thy inches, thou shouldst know
There were a heart in Egypt.

ANTONY: Hear me Queen:
  The strong necessity of Time, commands
  Our services awhile: but my full heart
  Remains in use with you. Our Italy,
  Shines o'er with civil swords; Sextus Pompeius
  Makes his approaches to the Port of Rome,
  Equality of two domestic powers,
  Breed scrupulous faction: the hated grown to strength
  Are newly grown to love: the condemn'd Pompey,
  Rich in his father's honour, creeps apace
  Into the hearts of such, as have not thrived
  Upon the present state, whose numbers threaten,
  And quietness grown sick of rest, would purge
  By any desperate change: my more particular,
  And that which most with you should safe my going,
  Is Fulvia's death.

CLEOPATRA: Though age from folly could not give me
    freedom
  It does from childishness. Can Fulvia die?

ANTONY: She's dead my Queen.
  Look here, and at thy sovereign leisure read
  The garboils she awak'd: at the last, best,
  See when, and where she died.

CLEOPATRA: O most false love!
  Where be the sacred vials thou shouldst fill

With sorrowful water? Now I see, I see,
In Fulvia's death, how mine receiv'd shall be.
ANTONY: Quarrel no more, but be prepar'd to know
The purposes I bear: which are, or cease,
As you shall give th' advice. By the fire
That quickens Nilus' slime, I go from hence
Thy soldier, servant, making peace or war,
As thou affects.
CLEOPATRA: Cut my lace, Charmian come,
But let it be, I am quickly ill, and well,
So Antony loves.
ANTONY: My precious Queen forbear,
And give true evidence to his love, which stands
An honourable trial.
CLEOPATRA: So Fulvia told me.
I prithee turn aside, and weep for her,
Then bid adieu to me, and say the tears
Belong to Egypt. Good now, play one scene
Of excellent dissembling, and let it look
Like perfect honour.
ANTONY: You'll heat my blood, no more!
CLEOPATRA: You can do better yet: but this is meetly.
ANTONY: Now by sword.
CLEOPATRA: And target. Still he mends.
But this is not the best. Look prithee Charmian,
How this Herculean Roman does become
The carriage of his chafe.
ANTONY: I'll leave you Lady.
CLEOPATRA: Courteous Lord, one word:
Sir, you and I must part, but that's not it:
Sir, you and I have lov'd, but there's not it:
That you know well, something it is I would:
Oh, my oblivion is a very Antony,

And I am all forgotten.

ANTONY: But that your royalty
  Holds idleness your subject, I should take you
  For idleness itself.

CLEOPATRA: 'Tis sweating labour,
  To bear such idleness so near the heart
  As Cleopatra this. But sir, forgive me,
  Since my becomings kill me, when they do not
  Eye well to you. Your honour calls you hence,
  Therefore be deaf to my unpitied folly,
  And all the Gods go with you. Upon your sword
  Sit laurel victory, and smooth success
  Be strew'd before your feet.

ANTONY: Let us go.
  Come: our separation so abides and flies,
  That thou residing here, go'st yet with me:
  And I hence fleeting, here remain with thee.
  Away.

Exeunt.

I. 4

Enter Octavius reading a letter, Lepidus, and their train.

CÆSAR: You may see Lepidus, and henceforth know,
  It is not Cæsar's natural vice, to hate
  Our great competitor. From Alexandria
  This is the news: he fishes, drinks, and wastes
  The lamps of night in revel: is not more manlike
  Than Cleopatra: nor the Queen of Ptolemy
  More womanly than he. Hardly gave audience
  Or vouchsafe'd to think he had partners. You
  Shall find there a man, who is th' abstract of all faults,
  That all men follow.

LEPIDUS: I must not think
There are, evils enow to darken all his goodness:
His faults in him, seem as the spots of Heaven,
More fiery by night's blackness; hereditary,
Rather than purchas'd: what he cannot change,
Than what he chooses.

CÆSAR: You are too indulgent. Let's grant it is not
Amiss to tumble on the bed of Ptolemy,
To give a Kingdom for a mirth, to sit
And keep the turn of tippling with a slave,
To reel the streets at noon, and stand the buffet
With knaves that smells of sweat: say this becomes him
(As his composure must be rare indeed,
Whom these things cannot blemish) yet must Antony
No way excuse his soils, when we do bear
So great weight in his lightness. If he fill'd
His vacancy with his voluptuousness,
Full surfeits, and the dryness of his bones,
Call on him for 't. But to confound such time,
That drums him from his sport, and speaks as loud
As his own State, and ours, 'tis to be chid:
As we rate boys, who being mature in knowledge,
Pawn their experience to their present pleasure,
And so rebel to judgement.

Enter a Messenger.

LEPIDUS: Here 's more news.

MESSENGER: Thy biddings have been done, and every
hour
Most noble Cæsar, shalt thou have report
How 'tis abroad. Pompey is strong at sea,
And it appears, he is belov'd of those
That only have fear'd Cæsar: to the ports
The discontents repair, and men's reports

Give him much wrong'd.

CÆSAR: I should have known no less,
It hath been taught us from the primal state
That he which is was wish'd, until he were:
And the ebb'd man,
Ne'er lov'd, till ne'er worth love,
Comes fear'd by being lack'd. This common body,
Like to a vagabond flag upon the stream,
Goes to, and back, lacking the varying tide
To rot itself with motion.

MESSENGER: Cæsar, I bring thee word,
Menecrates and Menas famous pirates,
Makes the sea serve them, which they ear and wound
With keels of every kind. Many hot inroads
They make in Italy, the borders maritime
Lack blood to think on 't, and flush youth revolt,
No vessel can peep forth: but 'tis as soon
Taken as seen: for Pompey's name strikes more
Than could his war resisted.

CÆSAR: Antony,
Leave thy lascivious wassails. When thou once
Was beaten from Modena, where thou slew'st
Hirtius and Pansa Consuls, at thy heel
Did Famine follow, whom thou fought'st against,
(Though daintily brought up) with patience more
Than savages could suffer. Thou didst drink
The stale of horses, and the gilded puddle
Which beasts would cough at. Thy palate then did deign
The roughest berry, on the rudest hedge.
Yea, like the stag, when snow the pasture sheets,
The barks of trees thou brows'd. On the Alps,
It is reported thou didst eat strange flesh,
Which some did die to look on: and all this

(It wounds thine honour that I speak it now)
Was borne so like a soldier, that thy cheek
So much as lank'd not.

LEPIDUS: 'Tis pity of him.

CÆSAR: Let his shames quickly
Drive him to Rome, 'tis time we twain
Did show ourselves i' th' field, and to that end
Assemble me immediate council, Pompey
Thrives in our idleness.

LEPIDUS: To-morrow Cæsar,
I shall be furnish'd to inform you rightly
Both what by sea and land I can be able
To front this present time.

CÆSAR: Till which encounter, it is my business too.
Farewell.

LEPIDUS: Farewell my Lord, what you shall know meantime
Of stirs abroad, I shall beseech you Sir,
To let me be partaker.

CÆSAR: Doubt not sir, I knew it for my bond.

Exeunt.

I. 5

Enter Cleopatra, Charmian, Iras, and Mardian.

CLEOPATRA: Charmian.

CHARMIAN: Madam.

CLEOPATRA: Ha, ha, give me to drink mandragora.

CHARMIAN: Why, Madam?

CLEOPATRA: That I might sleep out this great gap of
time:
My Antony is away.

CHARMIAN: You think of him too much.

CLEOPATRA: O 'tis treason.

CHARMIAN: Madam, I trust not so.

CLEOPATRA: Thou, Eunuch Mardian.

MARDIAN: What 's your Highness' pleasure?

CLEOPATRA: Not now to hear thee sing, I take no pleasure
In aught an eunuch has: 'tis well for thee,
That being unseminar'd, thy freer thoughts
May not fly forth of Egypt. Hast thou affections?

MARDIAN: Yes, gracious Madam.

CLEOPATRA: Indeed?

MARDIAN: Not in deed Madam, for I can do nothing
But what in deed is honest to be done:
Yet have I fierce affections, and think
What Venus did with Mars.

CLEOPATRA: Oh Charmian:
Where think'st thou he is now? Stands he, or sits he?
Or does he walk? or is he on his horse?
Oh happy horse to bear the weight of Antony!
Do bravely horse, for wot'st thou whom thou mov'st,
The demi-Atlas of this Earth, the arm
And burgonet of men. He's speaking now,
Or murmuring, where 's my serpent of old Nile,
(For so he calls me). Now I feed myself
With most delicious poison. Think on me
That am with Phœbus' amorous pinches black,
And wrinkled deep in time. Broad-fronted Cæsar,
When thou wast here above the ground, I was
A morsel for a Monarch: and great Pompey
Would stand and make his eyes grow in my brow,
There would he anchor his aspect, and die
With looking on his life.

Enter Alexas from Antony.

ALEXAS: Sovereign of Egypt, hail.

CLEOPATRA: How much unlike art thou Mark Antony?
  Yet coming from him, that great medicine hath
  With his tinct gilded thee.
  How goes it with my brave Mark Antony?
ALEXAS: Last thing he did (dear Queen)
  He kiss'd the last of many doubled kisses
  This orient pearl. His speech sticks in my heart.
CLEOPATRA: Mine ear must pluck it thence.
ALEXAS: Good friend, quoth he:
  Say the firm Roman to great Egypt sends
  This treasure of an oyster: at whose foot
  To mend the petty present, I will piece
  Her opulent Throne, with Kingdoms. All the East,
  (Say thou) shall call her Mistress. So he nodded,
  And soberly did mount an arm-gaunt steed,
  Who neigh'd so high, that what I would have spoke,
  Was beastly dumb'd by him.
CLEOPATRA: What was he sad, or merry?
ALEXAS: Like to the time o' th' year, between the extremes
  Of hot and cold, he was nor sad nor merry.
CLEOPATRA: Oh well divided disposition: note him,
  Note him good Charmian, 'tis the man; but note him.
  He was not sad, for he would shine on those
  That make their looks by his. He was not merry,
  Which seem'd to tell them, his remembrance lay
  In Egypt with his joy, but between both.
  Oh heavenly mingle! Be'st thou sad, or merry,
  The violence of either thee becomes,
  So does it no man else. Met'st thou my posts?
ALEXAS: Ay Madam, twenty several messengers.
  Why do you send so thick?
CLEOPATRA: Who 's born that day, when I forget to
  send to Antony, shall die a beggar. Ink and paper

Charmian. Welcome my good Alexas. Did I Charmian,
ever love Cæsar so?

CHARMIAN: Oh that brave Cæsar!

CLEOPATRA: Be chok'd with such another emphasis,
Say the brave Antony.

CHARMIAN: The valiant Cæsar.

CLEOPATRA: By Isis, I will give thee bloody teeth,
If thou with Cæsar paragon again:
My man of men.

CHARMIAN: By your most gracious pardon,
I sing but after you.

CLEOPATRA: My salad days,
When I was green in judgement, cold in blood,
To say, as I said then. But come, away,
Get me ink and paper,
He shall have every day a several greeting, or I'll un-
people Egypt.

Exeunt.

II. 1

Enter Pompey, Menecrates, and Menas, in warlike manner.

POMPEY: If the great Gods be just, they shall assist
The deeds of justest men.

MENECRATES: Know worthy Pompey, that what they do
delay, they not deny.

POMPEY: Whiles we are suitors to their throne, decays the
thing we sue for.

MENECRATES: We ignorant of ourselves,
Beg often our own harms, which the wise Powers
Deny us for our good: so find we profit
By losing of our prayers.

POMPEY: I shall do well:

The people love me, and the sea is mine;
My powers are crescent, and my auguring hope
Says it will come to th' full. Mark Antony
In Egypt sits at dinner, and will make
No wars without doors. Cæsar gets money where
He loses hearts: Lepidus ſlatters both,
Of both is flatter'd: but he neither loves,
Nor either cares for him.

MENAS: Cæsar and Lepidus are in the field,
A mighty strength they carry.

POMPEY: Where have you this? 'Tis false.

MENAS: From Silvius, Sir.

POMPEY: He dreams: I know they are in Rome together
Looking for Antony: but all the charms of love,
Salt Cleopatra soften thy wan'd lip,
Let Witchcraft join with Beauty, Lust with both,
Tie up the libertine in a field of feasts,
Keep his brain fuming. Epicurean cooks,
Sharpen with cloyless sauce his appetite,
That sleep and feeding may prorogue his honour,
Even till a Lethe'd dulness —

Enter Varrius.

How now Varrius?

VARRIUS: This is most certain, that I shall deliver:
Mark Antony is every hour in Rome
Expected. Since he went from Egypt, 'tis
A space for farther travel.

POMPEY: I could have given less matter
A better ear. Menas, I did not think
This amorous surfeiter would have donn'd his helm
For such a petty war: his soldiership
Is twice the other twain: but let us rear
The higher our opinion, that our stirring

Can from the lap of Egypt's widow, pluck
The ne'er lust-wearied Antony.

MENAS: I cannot hope,
Cæsar and Antony shall well greet together;
His wife that's dead, did trespasses to Cæsar,
His brother warr'd upon him, although I think
Not mov'd by Antony.

POMPEY: I know not Menas,
How lesser enmities may give way to greater,
Were 't not that we stand up against them all:
'Twere pregnant they should square between themselves,
For they have entertained cause enough
To draw their swords: but how the fear of us
May cement their divisions, and bind up
The petty difference, we yet not know:
Be't as our gods will have 't; it only stands
Our lives upon, to use our strongest hands.
Come Menas.

Exeunt.

II. 2

Enter Enobarbus and Lepidus.

LEPIDUS: Good Enobarbus, 'tis a worthy deed,
And shall become you well, to entreat your Captain
To soft and gentle speech.

ENOBARBUS: I shall entreat him
To answer like himself: if Cæsar move him,
Let Antony look over Cæsar's head,
And speak as loud as Mars. By Jupiter,
Were I the wearer of Antonius' beard,
I would not shave 't to-day.

LEPIDUS: 'Tis not a time for private stomaching.

ENOBARBUS: Every time serves for the matter that is then
 born in 't.

LEPIDUS: But small to greater matters must give way.

ENOBARBUS: Not if the small come first.

LEPIDUS: Your speech is passion: but pray you stir
 No embers up. Here comes the noble Antony.

Enter Antony and Ventidius.

ENOBARBUS: And yonder Cæsar.

Enter Cæsar, Mæcenas, and Agrippa.

ANTONY: If we compose well here, to Parthia:
 Hark Ventidius.

CÆSAR: I do not know Mæcenas, ask Agrippa.

LEPIDUS: Noble friends:
 That which combin'd us was most great, and let not
 A leaner action rend us. What 's amiss,
 May it be gently heard. When we debate
 Our trivial difference loud, we do commit
 Murther in healing wounds. Then noble partners,
 The rather for I earnestly beseech,
 Touch you the sourest points with sweetest terms,
 Nor curstness grow to th' matter.

ANTONY: 'Tis spoken well:
 Were we before our armies, and to fight,
 I should do thus.

Flourish.

CÆSAR: Welcome to Rome.

ANTONY: Thank you.

CÆSAR: Sit.

ANTONY: Sit sir.

CÆSAR: Nay then.

ANTONY: I learn, you take things ill, which are not so:
 Or being, concern you not.

CÆSAR: I must be laugh'd at, if or for nothing, or a little, I
　　Should say myself offended, and with you
　　Chiefly i' th' world. More laugh'd at, that I should
　　Once name you derogately: when to sound your name
　　It not concern'd me.

ANTONY: My being in Egypt Cæsar, what was 't to you?

CÆSAR: No more than my residing here at Rome
　　Might be to you in Egypt: yet if you there
　　Did practise on my State, your being in Egypt
　　Might be my question,

ANTONY: How intend you, practis'd?

CÆSAR: You may be pleas'd to catch at mine intent,
　　By what did here befal me. Your wife and brother
　　Made wars upon me and their contestation
　　Was theme for you, you were the word of war.

ANTONY: You do mistake your business, my brother
　　never
　　Did urge me in his act: I did inquire it,
　　And have my learning from some true reports
　　That drew their swords with you, did he not rather
　　Discredit my authority with yours,
　　And make the wars alike against my stomach,
　　Having alike your cause? Of this, my letters
　　Before did satisfy you. If you'll patch a quarrel,
　　As matter whole you have to make it with,
　　It must not be with this.

CÆSAR: You praise yourself, by laying defects of judge-
　　ment to me: but you patch'd up your excuses.

ANTONY: Not so, not so:
　　I know you could not lack, I am certain on 't,
　　Very necessity of this thought, that I
　　Your partner in the cause 'gainst which he fought,
　　Could not with graceful eyes attend those wars

Which fronted mine own peace. As for my wife,
I would you had her spirit, in such another,
The third o' th' world is yours, which with a snaffle,
You may pace easy, but not such a wife.

ENOBARBUS: Would we had all such wives, that the men
might go to wars with the women.

ANTONY: So much uncurbable, her garboils (Cæsar)
Made out of her impatience: which not wanted
Shrewdness of policy too: I grieving grant,
Did you too much disquiet, for that you must,
But say I could not help it.

CÆSAR: I wrote to you, when rioting in Alexandria, you
Did pocket up my letters: and with taunts
Did gibe my missive out of audience.

ANTONY: Sir, he fell upon me, ere admitted, then:
Three Kings I had newly feasted, and did want
Of what I was i' th' morning: but next day
I told him of myself, which was as much
As to have ask'd him pardon. Let this fellow
Be nothing of our strife: if we contend
Out of our question wipe him.

CÆSAR: You have broken the article of your oath, which
you shall never have tongue to charge me with.

LEPIDUS: Soft Cæsar.

ANTONY: No Lepidus, let him speak,
The honour is sacred which he talks on now,
Supposing that I lack'd it: but on Cæsar,
The article of my oath.

CÆSAR: To lend me arms, and aid when I requir'd them,
The which you both denied.

ANTONY: Neglected rather:
And then when poisoned hours had bound me up
From mine own knowledge, as nearly as I may,

I'll play the penitent to you. But mine honesty,
Shall not make poor my greatness, nor my power
Work without it. Truth is, that Fulvia,
To have me out of Egypt, made wars here,
For which myself, the ignorant motive, do
So far ask pardon, as befits mine honour
To stoop in such a case.

LEPIDUS: 'Tis noble spoken.

MÆCENAS: If it might please you, to enforce no further
The griefs between ye: to forget them quite,
Were to remember that the present need,
Speaks to atone you.

LEPIDUS: Worthily spoken Mæcenas.

ENOBARBUS: Or if you borrow one another's love for
the instant, you may when you hear no more words of
Pompey return it again: you shall have time to wrangle
in, when you have nothing else to do.

ANTONY: Thou art a soldier, only speak no more.

ENOBARBUS: That truth should be silent, I had almost
forgot.

ANTONY: You wrong this presence, therefore speak no
more.

ENOBARBUS: Go to then: your considerate stone.

CÆSAR: I do not much dislike the matter, but
The manner of his speech: for 't cannot be,
We shall remain in friendship, our conditions
So diff'ring in their acts. Yet if I knew,
What hoop should hold us stanch from edge to edge
A' th' world, I would pursue it.

AGRIPPA: Give me leave Cæsar.

CÆSAR: Speak Agrippa.

AGRIPPA: Thou hast a sister by the mother's side, admir'd
Octavia: great Mark Antony is now a widower.

CÆSAR: Say not, say Agrippa; if Cleopatra heard you,
your reproof were well deserved of rashness.

ANTONY: I am not married Cæsar: let me hear Agrippa
further speak.

AGRIPPA: To hold you in perpetual amity,
To make you brothers, and to knit your hearts
With an unslipping knot, take Antony,
Octavia to his wife: whose beauty claims
No worse a husband than the best of men: whose
Virtue, and whose general graces, speak
That which none else can utter. By this marriage,
All little jealousies which now seem great,
And all great fears, which now import their dangers,
Would then be nothing. Truths would be tales,
Where now half tales be truths: her love to both,
Would each to other, and all loves to both
Draw after her. Pardon what I have spoke,
For 'tis a studied not a present thought,
By duty ruminated.

ANTONY: Will Cæsar speak?

CÆSAR: Not till he hears how Antony is touch'd,
With what is spoke already.

ANTONY: What power is in Agrippa,
If I would say Agrippa, be it so,
To make this good?

CÆSAR: The power of Cæsar,
And his power, unto Octavia.

ANTONY: May I never
(To this good purpose, that so fairly shows)
Dream of impediment: let me have thy hand:
Further this act of grace: and from this hour,
The heart of brothers govern in our loves,
And sway our great designs.

CÆSAR: There's my hand:
  A sister I bequeath you, whom no brother
  Did ever love so dearly. Let her live
  To join our kingdoms, and our hearts, and never
  Fly off our loves again.
LEPIDUS: Happily, Amen.
ANTONY: I did not think to draw my sword 'gainst
      Pompey,
  For he hath laid strange courtesies, and great
  Of late upon me. I must thank him only,
  Lest my remembrance, suffer ill report:
  At heel of that, defy him.
LEPIDUS: Time calls upon 's,
  Of us must Pompey presently be sought,
  Or else he seeks out us.
ANTONY: Where lies he?
CÆSAR: About the Mount Misenum.
ANTONY: What is his strength by land?
CÆSAR: Great, and increasing:
  But by sea he is an absolute master.
ANTONY: So is the fame.
  Would we had spoke together. Haste we for it,
  Yet ere we put ourselves in arms, dispatch we
  The business we have talk'd of.
CÆSAR: With most gladness,
  And do invite you to my sister's view,
  Whither straight I'll lead you.
ANTONY: Let us Lepidus, not lack your company.
LEPIDUS: Noble Antony, not sickness should detain
  me.

            Flourish. Exeunt omnes.
        Manent Enobarbus, Agrippa, Mæcenas.
MÆCENAS: Welcome from Egypt, Sir.

ENOBARBUS: Half the heart of Cæsar, worthy Mæcenas.
My honourable friend Agrippa.

AGRIPPA: Good Enobarbus.

MÆCENAS: We have cause to be glad, that matters are
so well digested: you stay'd well by 't in Egypt.

ENOBARBUS: Ay Sir, we did sleep day out of countenance:
and made the night light with drinking.

MÆCENAS: Eight wild-boars roasted whole at a break-
fast: and but twelve persons there. Is this true?

ENOBARBUS: This was but as a fly by an eagle: we had
much more monstrous matter of feast, which worthily
deserved noting.

MÆCENAS: She 's a most triumphant Lady, if report be
square to her.

ENOBARBUS: When she first met Mark Antony, she purs'd
up his heart upon the River of Cydnus.

AGRIPPA: There she appear'd indeed: or my reporter
devis'd well for her.

ENOBARBUS: I will tell you,
The barge she sat in, like a burnish'd Throne
Burnt on the water: the poop was beaten gold,
Purple the sails: and so perfumed that
The winds were love-sick.
With them the oars were silver,
Which to the tune of flutes kept stroke, and made
The water which they beat, to follow faster;
As amorous of their strokes. For her own person,
It beggar'd all description, she did lie
In her pavilion, cloth of gold, of tissue,
O'er-picturing that Venus, where we see
The fancy out-work Nature. On each side her,
Stood pretty dimpled boys, like smiling Cupids,
With divers colour'd fans whose wind did seem,

To glow the delicate cheeks which they did cool,
And what they undid did.

AGRIPPA: Oh rare for Antony.

ENOBARBUS: Her gentlewomen, like the Nereides,
So many mermaids tended her i' th' eyes,
And made their bends adornings. At the helm,
A seeming mermaid steers: the silken tackle,
Swell with the touches of those flower-soft hands,
That yarely frame the office. From the barge
A strange invisible perfume hits the sense
Of the adjacent wharfs. The city cast
Her people out upon her: and Antony
Enthron'd i' th' market-place, did sit alone,
Whistling to th' air: which but for vacancy,
Had gone to gaze on Cleopatra too,
And made a gap in Nature.

AGRIPPA: Rare Egyptian.

ENOBARBUS: Upon her landing, Antony sent to her,
Invited her to supper: she replied,
It should be better, he became her guest:
Which she entreated, our courteous Antony,
Whom ne'er the word of no woman heard speak,
Being barber'd ten times o'er, goes to the feast:
And for his ordinary, pays his heart,
For what his eyes eat only.

AGRIPPA: Royal wench:
She made great Cæsar lay his sword to bed,
He plough'd her, and she cropp'd.

ENOBARBUS: I saw her once
Hop forty paces through the public street,
And having lost her breath, she spoke, and panted,
That she did make defect, perfection,
And breathless power breathe forth.

MÆCENAS: Now Antony must leave her utterly.

ENOBARBUS: Never he will not:
  Age cannot wither her, nor custom stale
  Her infinite variety: other women cloy
  The appetites they feed, but she makes hungry,
  Where most she satisfies. For vilest things
  Become themselves in her, that the holy Priests
  Bless her, when she is riggish.

MÆCENAS: If beauty, wisdom, modesty, can settle
  The heart of Antony, Octavia is
  A blessed lottery to him.

AGRIPPA: Let us go. Good Enobarbus, make yourself my
  guest, whilst you abide here.

ENOBARBUS: Humbly Sir I thank you.

Exeunt.

II. 3

Enter Antony, Cæsar, Octavia between them.

ANTONY: The world, and my great office, will
  Sometimes divide me from your bosom.

OCTAVIA: All which time, before the Gods my knee shall
  bow my prayers to them for you.

ANTONY: Good night Sir. My Octavia
  Read not my blemishes in the world's report:
  I have not kept my square, but that to come
  Shall all be done by th' rule: good night dear Lady:
  Good night Sir.

CÆSAR: Good night.

Exeunt all but Antony.

Enter Soothsayer.

ANTONY: Now sirrah: you do wish yourself in Egypt?

SOOTHSAYER: Would I had never come from thence, nor
    you thither.
ANTONY: If you can, your reason?
SOOTHSAYER: I see it in my motion, have it not in my
    tongue,
But yet hie you to Egypt again.
ANTONY: Say to me, whose fortunes shall rise higher,
    Cæsar's or mine?
SOOTHSAYER: Cæsar's. Therefore, oh Antony, stay not
    by his side:
Thy demon, that thy spirit which keeps thee, is
Noble, courageous, high unmatchable,
Where Cæsar's is not. But near him, thy angel
Becomes a fear, as being o'erpower'd: therefore
Make space enough between you.
ANTONY: Speak this no more.
SOOTHSAYER: To none but thee, no more but when to
    thee:
If thou dost play with him at any game,
Thou art sure to lose: and of that natural luck,
He beats thee 'gainst the odds. Thy lustre thickens,
When he shines by: I say again, thy spirit
Is all afraid to govern thee near him:
But he away 'tis noble.
ANTONY: Get thee gone:
Say to Ventidius I would speak with him.
                    Exit Soothsayer.
He shall to Parthis. Be it art or hap,
He hath spoken true. The very dice obey him,
And in our sports my better cunning faints,
Under his chance; if we draw lots he speeds,
His cocks do win the battle, still of mine,
When it is all to nought: and his quails ever

Beat mine (inhoop'd) at odds. I will to Egypt:
And though I make this marriage for my peace,
I' th' East my pleasure lies.
Oh come Ventidius.

Enter Ventidius.

You must to Parthia, your commission 's ready:
Follow me, and receive 't.

Exeunt.

II. 4

Enter Lepidus, Mæcenas, and Agrippa.

LEPIDUS: Trouble yourselves no further: pray you hasten
your Generals after.

AGRIPPA: Sir, Mark Antony, will e'en but kiss Octavia,
and we 'll follow.

LEPIDUS: Till I shall see you in your soldier's dress,
Which will become you both: farewell.

MÆCENAS: We shall, as I conceive the journey, be at the
Mount before you Lepidus.

LEPIDUS: Your way is shorter, my purposes do draw me
much about, you'll win two days upon me.

BOTH: Sir good success.

LEPIDUS: Farewell.

Exeunt.

II. 5

Enter Cleopatra, Charmian, Iras, and Alexas.

CLEOPATRA: Give me some music: music, moody food
Of us that trade in love.

ALL: The music, hoa.

Enter Mardian the Eunuch.

CLEOPATRA: Let it alone, let 's to billiards: come Charmian.

CHARMIAN: My arm is sore, best play with Mardian.

CLEOPATRA: As well a woman with an eunuch play'd, as
   with a woman. Come you'll play with me Sir?

MARDIAN: As well as I can Madam.

CLEOPATRA: And when good will is showed,
   Though 't come too short
   The actor may plead pardon. I'll none now,
   Give me mine angle, we 'll to th' river there,
   My music playing far off. I will betray
   Tawny fine fishes, my bended hook shall pierce
   Their slimy jaws: and as I draw them up,
   I'll think them every one an Antony,
   And say, ah ha; y'are caught.

CHARMIAN: 'Twas merry when you wager'd on your
   angling, when your diver did hang a salt fish on his hook
   which he with fervency drew up.

CLEOPATRA: That time? Oh times:
   I laugh'd him out of patience: and that night
   I laugh'd him into patience, and next morn,
   Ere the ninth hour, I drunk him to his bed:
   Then put my tires and mantles on him, whilst
   I wore his sword Philippan. Oh from Italy.

                    Enter a Messenger.
   Ram thou thy fruitful tidings in mine ears,
   That long time have been barren.

MESSENGER: Madam, Madam.

CLEOPATRA: Antony's dead.
   If thou say so villain, thou kill'st thy Mistress:
   But well and free, if thou so yield him,
   There is gold, and here
   My bluest veins to kiss: a hand that Kings

Have lipp'd, and trembled kissing.

MESSENGER: First Madam, he is well.

CLEOPATRA: Why there's more gold.
But sirrah mark, we use
To say, the dead are well: bring it to that,
The gold I give thee, will I melt and pour
Down thy ill uttering throat.

MESSENGER: Good Madam hear me.

CLEOPATRA: Well, go to I will:
But there 's no goodness in thy face if Antony
Be free and healthful; so tart a favour
To trumpet such good tidings. If not well,
Thou shouldst come like a Fury crown'd with snakes,
Not like a formal man.

MESSENGER: Will 't please you hear me?

CLEOPATRA: I have a mind to strike thee ere thou speak'st:
Yet if thou say Antony lives, 'tis well,
Or friends with Cæsar, or not captive to him,
I'll set thee in a shower of gold, and hail
Rich pearls upon thee.

MESSENGER: Madam, he's well.

CLEOPATRA: Well said.

MESSENGER: And friends with Cæsar.

CLEOPATRA: Thou'rt an honest man.

MESSENGER: Cæsar, and he, are greater friends than ever.

CLEOPATRA: Make thee a fortune from me.

MESSENGER: But yet Madam.

CLEOPATRA: I do not like but yet, it does allay
The good precedence, fie upon but yet,
But yet is as a gaoler to bring forth
Some monstrous malefactor. Prithee friend,
Pour out the pack of matter to mine ear,
The good and bad together: he's friends with Cæsar,

In state of health thou say'st, and thou say'st, free.

MESSENGER: Free Madam, no: I made no such report,
  He 's bound unto Octavia.

CLEOPATRA: For what good turn?

MESSENGER: For the best turn i' th' bed.

CLEOPATRA: I am pale Charmian.

MESSENGER: Madam, he's married to Octavia.

CLEOPATRA: The most infectious pestilence upon thee.
                                    Strikes him down.

MESSENGER: Good Madam patience.

CLEOPATRA: What say you?
                                    Strikes him.
  Hence horrible villain, or I'll spurn thine eyes
  Like balls before me: I'll unhair thy head,
                    She hales him up and down.
  Thou shalt be whipp'd with wire, and stew'd in brine,
  Smarting in ling'ring pickle.

MESSENGER: Gracious Madam,
  I that do bring the news, made not the match.

CLEOPATRA: Say 'tis not so, a Province I will give thee,
  And make thy fortunes proud: the blow thou hadst
  Shall make thy peace, for moving me to rage,
  And I will boot thee with what gift beside
  Thy modesty can beg.

MESSENGER: He's married Madam.

CLEOPATRA: Rogue, thou hast liv'd too long. *Draws a
  knife.*

MESSENGER: Nay then I'll run:
  What mean you Madam, I have made no fault.
                                    Exit.

CHARMIAN: Good Madam, keep yourself within yourself,
  The man is innocent.

CLEOPATRA: Some innocents 'scape not the thunderbolt:

Melt Egypt into Nile: and kindly creatures
Turn all to serpents. Call the slave again,
Though I am mad, I will not bite him: call!

CHARMIAN: He is afeard to come.

CLEOPATRA: I will not hurt him,
These hands do lack nobility, that they strike
A meaner than myself: since I myself
Have given myself the cause. Come hither Sir.

Enter the Messenger again.

Though it be honest, it is never good
To bring bad news: give to a gracious message
An host of tongues, but let ill tidings tell
Themselves, when they be felt.

MESSENGER: I have done my duty.

CLEOPATRA: Is he married?
I cannot hate thee worser than I do,
If thou again say yes.

MESSENGER: He's married, Madam.

CLEOPATRA: The Gods confound thee,
Dost thou hold there still?

MESSENGER: Should I lie Madam?

CLEOPATRA: Oh, I would thou didst:
So half my Egypt were submerg'd and made
A cistern for scal'd snakes. Go get thee hence.
Hadst thou Narcissus in thy face, to me
Thou wouldst appear most ugly: he is married?

MESSENGER: I crave your Highness' pardon.

CLEOPATRA: He is married?

MESSENGER: Take no offence, that I would not offend you,
To punish me for what you make me do
Seems much unequal, he's married to Octavia.

CLEOPATRA: Oh that his fault should make a knave of thee,
That art not what th' art sure of. Get thee hence,

The merchandise which thou hast brought from Rome
Are all too dear for me:
Lie they upon thy hand, and be undone by 'em.
                    Exit Messenger.
CHARMIAN: Good your Highness patience.
CLEOPATRA: In praising Antony, I have disprais'd Cæsar.
CHARMIAN: Many times, Madam.
CLEOPATRA: I am paid for 't now: lead me from hence,
I faint, oh Iras, Charmian: 'tis no matter.
Go to the fellow, good Alexas bid him
Report the feature of Octavia: her years,
Her inclination, let him not leave out,
The colour of her hair. Bring me word quickly.
                    Exit Alexas.
Let him for ever go, let him not Charmian,
Though he be painted one way like a Gorgon,
The other way 's a Mars. Bid you Alexas
Bring me word, how tall she is: pity me Charmian,
But do not speak to me. Lead me to my chamber.
                    Exeunt.

II. 6

Flourish. Enter Pompey at one door, with drum and trumpet
at another Cæsar, Lepidus, Antony, Enobarbus, Mæcenas,
Agrippa, Menas, with Soldiers marching.
POMPEY: Your hostages I have, so have you mine:
And we shall talk before we fight.
CÆSAR: Most meet that first we come to words,
And therefore have we
Our written purposes before us sent,
Which if thou hast considered, let us know,
If 'twill tie up thy discontented sword,

And carry back to Sicily much tall youth,
That else must perish here.
POMPEY: To you all three,
The Senators alone of this great world,
Chief factors for the Gods. I do not know,
Wherefore my father should revengers want,
Having a son and friends, since Julius Cæsar,
Who at Philippi the good Brutus ghosted,
There saw you labouring for him. What was 't
That mov'd pale Cassius to conspire? And what
Made all-honour'd, honest, Roman Brutus,
With the arm'd rest, courtiers of beauteous freedom,
To drench the Capitol but that they would
Have one man but a man, and that is it
Hath made me rig my navy, at whose burthen,
The anger'd ocean foams, with which I meant
To scourge th' ingratitude, that despiteful Rome
Cast on my noble father.
CÆSAR: Take your time.
ANTONY: Thou canst not fear us Pompey with thy sails
We'll speak with thee at sea. At land thou know'st
How much we do o'ercount thee.
POMPEY: At land indeed
Thou dost o'ercount me of my father's house:
But since the cuckoo builds not for himself,
Remain in 't as thou mayst.
LEPIDUS: Be pleas'd to tell us,
(For this is from the present) how you take
The offers we have sent you.
CÆSAR: There's the point.
ANTONY: Which do not be entreated to:
But weigh what it is worth embrac'd.
CÆSAR: And what may follow to try a larger fortune.

POMPEY: You have made me offer
  Of Sicily, Sardinia: and I must
  Rid all the sea of pirates. Then, to send
  Measures of wheat to Rome: this 'greed upon,
  To part with unhack'd edges, and bear back
  Our targes undinted.

ALL: That's our offer.

POMPEY: Know then I came before you here,
  A man prepared
  To take this offer. But Mark Antony,
  Put me to some impatience: though I lose
  The praise of it by telling. You must know
  When Cæsar and your brother were at blows,
  Your mother came to Sicily, and did find
  Her welcome friendly.

ANTONY: I have heard it Pompey,
  And am well studied for a liberal thanks,
  Which I do owe you.

POMPEY: Let me have your hand:
  I did not think Sir, to have met you here.

ANTONY: The beds i' th' East are soft, and thanks to you,
  That call'd me timelier than my purpose hither:
  For I have gain'd by 't.

CÆSAR: Since I saw you last, there's a change upon you.

POMPEY: Well, I know not,
  What counts harsh Fortune casts upon my face,
  But in my bosom shall she never come,
  To make my heart her vassal.

LEPIDUS: Well met here.

POMPEY: I hope so Lepidus, thus we are agreed:
  I crave our composition may be written
  And seal'd between us.

CÆSAR: That's the next to do.

POMPEY: We 'll feast each other, ere we part, and let's
  Draw lots who shall begin.

ANTONY: That will I Pompey.

POMPEY: No, Antony take the lot: but first or last, your
  fine Egyptian cookery shall have the fame, I have heard
  that Julius Cæsar, grew fat with feasting there.

ANTONY: You have heard much.

POMPEY: I have fair meaning Sir.

ANTONY: And fair words to them.

POMPEY: Then so much have I heard,
  And I have heard Apollodorus carried –

ENOBARBUS: No more of that: he did so.

POMPEY: What I pray you?

ENOBARBUS: A certain Queen to Cæsar in a mattress.

POMPEY: I know thee now, how far'st thou soldier?

ENOBARBUS: Well, and well am like to do, for I perceive
  Four feasts are toward.

POMPEY: Let me shake thy hand,
  I never hated thee: I have seen thee fight,
  When I have envied thy behaviour.

ENOBARBUS: Sir, I never lov'd you much, but I ha' prais'd
  ye,
  When you have well deserv'd ten times as much,
  As I have said you did.

POMPEY: Enjoy thy plainness,
  It nothing ill becomes thee:
  Aboard my galley, I invite you all.
  Will you lead, Lords?

ALL: Show 's the way, Sir

POMPEY: Come.

  Exeunt. Manent Enobarbus and Menas.

MENAS: Thy father Pompey would ne'er have made this
  Treaty. You, and I have known, Sir.

ENOBARBUS: At sea, I think.

MENAS: We have Sir.

ENOBARBUS: You have done well by water.

MENAS: And you by land.

ENOBARBUS: I will praise any man that will praise me, though it cannot be denied what I have done by land.

MENAS: Nor what I have done by water.

ENOBARBUS: Yes something you can deny for your own safety: you have been a great thief by sea.

MENAS: And you by land.

ENOBARBUS: There I deny my land service: but give me your hand Menas, if our eyes had authority, here they might take two thieves kissing.

MENAS: All men's faces are true, whatsome'er their hands are.

ENOBARBUS: But there is never a fair woman, has a true face.

MENAS: No slander, they steal hearts.

ENOBARBUS: We came hither to fight with you.

MENAS: For my part, I am sorry it is turn'd to a drinking. Pompey doth this day laugh away his fortune.

ENOBARBUS: If he do, sure he cannot weep't back again.

MENAS: You 've said Sir, we look'd not for Mark Antony here, pray you, is he married to Cleopatra ?

ENOBARBUS: Cæsar's sister is call'd Octavia.

MENAS: True Sir, she was the wife of Caius Marcellus.

ENOBARBUS: But she is now the wife of Marcus Antonius.

MENAS: Pray ye Sir.

ENOBARBUS: 'Tis true.

MENAS: Then is Cæsar and he, for ever knit together.

ENOBARBUS: If I were bound to divine of this unity, I would not prophesy so.

MENAS: I think the policy of that purpose, made more in the marriage, than the love of the parties.

ENOBARBUS: I think so too. But you shall find the band that seems to tie their friendship together, will be the very strangler of their amity: Octavia is of a holy, cold, and still conversation.

MENAS: Who would not have his wife so?

ENOBARBUS: Not he that himself is not so: which is Mark Antony: he will to his Egyptian dish again: then shall the signs of Octavia blow the fire up in Cæsar, and (as I said before) that which is the strength of their amity, shall prove the immediate author of their variance. Antony will use his affection where it is. He married but his occasion here.

MENAS: And thus it may be. Come Sir, will you aboard? I have a health for you.

ENOBARBUS: I shall take it Sir: we have us'd our throats in Egypt.

MENAS: Come, let's away.

Exeunt.

II. 7

Music plays.
Enter two or three Servants with a banquet.

1 SERVANT: Here they 'll be man: some o' their plants are ill-rooted already, the least wind i' th' world will blow them down.

2 SERVANT: Lepidus is high-colour'd.

1 SERVANT: They have made him drink almsdrink.

2 SERVANT: As they pinch one another by the disposition, he cries out, no more; reconciles them to his entreaty, and himself to th' drink.

1 SERVANT: But it raises the greater war between him
and his discretion.

2 SERVANT: Why this it is to have a name in great men's
fellowship: I had as lief have a reed that will do me no
service, as a partisan I could not heave.

1 SERVANT: To be call'd into a huge sphere, and not to
be seen to move in 't, are the holes where eyes should
be, which pitifully disaster the cheeks.

A sennet sounded.

Enter Cæsar, Antony, Pompey, Lepidus, Agrippa, Mæcenas,
Enobarbus, Menas, with other Captains.

ANTONY: Thus do they Sir: they take the flow o' th' Nile
By certain scales i' th' Pyramid: they know
By th' height, the lowness, or the mean: if dearth
Or foison follow. The higher Nilus swells,
The more it promises: as it ebbs, the seedsman
Upon the slime and ooze scatters his grain,
And shortly comes to harvest.

LEPIDUS: You've strange serpents there?

ANTONY: Ay Lepidus.

LEPIDUS: Your serpent of Egypt, is bred now of your mud
by the operation of your sun: so is your crocodile.

ANTONY: They are so.

POMPEY: Sit, and some wine: a health to Lepidus.

LEPIDUS: I am not so well as I should be:
But I'll ne'er out.

ENOBARBUS: Not till you have slept: I fear me you'll be
in till then.

LEPIDUS: Nay certainly, I have heard the Ptolemies' pyra-
mises are very goodly things: without contradiction I
have heard that.

MENAS: Pompey, a word.

POMPEY: Say in mine ear, what is 't?

MENAS: Forsake thy seat I do beseech thee Captain,
  And hear me speak a word.
POMPEY: Forbear me till anon.
                    Whispers in's ear.
  This wine for Lepidus.
LEPIDUS: What manner o' thing is your crocodile?
ANTONY: It is shap'd Sir like itself, and it is as broad as
  it hath breadth; it is just so high as it is, and moves with
  it own organs. It lives by that which nourisheth it, and
  the elements once out of it, it transmigrates.
LEPIDUS: What colour is it of?
ANTONY: Of it own colour too.
LEPIDUS: 'Tis a strange serpent.
ANTONY: 'Tis so, and the tears of it are wet.
CÆSAR: Will this description satisfy him?
ANTONY: With the health that Pompey gives him, else
  he is a very epicure.
POMPEY: Go hang Sir, hang: tell me of that? Away:
  Do as I bid you. Where's this cup I call'd for?
MENAS: If for the sake of merit thou wilt hear me,
  Rise from thy stool.
POMPEY: I think thou 'rt mad: the matter?
MENAS: I have ever held my cap off to thy fortunes.
POMPEY: Thou hast serv'd me with much faith: what's
  else to say? Be jolly Lords.
ANTONY: These quick-sands Lepidus,
  Keep off them, for you sink.
MENAS: Wilt thou be Lord of all the world?
POMPEY: What say'st thou?
MENAS: Wilt thou be Lord of the whole world? That's
  twice.
POMPEY: How should that be?
MENAS: But entertain it, and though thou think me poor,

I am the man will give thee all the world.

POMPEY: Hast thou drunk well?

MENAS: No Pompey, I have kept me from the cup,
　　Thou art if thou dar'st be, the earthly Jove:
　　Whate'er the ocean pales, or sky inclips,
　　Is thine, if thou wilt ha 't.

POMPEY: Show me which way.

MENAS: These three World-sharers, these competitors
　　Are in thy vessel. Let me cut the cable,
　　And when we are put off, fall to their throats:
　　All there is thine.

POMPEY: Ah, this thou shouldst have done,
　　And not have spoke on 't. In me 'tis villainy,
　　In thee, 't had been good service: thou must know,
　　'Tis not my profit that does lead mine honour:
　　Mine honour it. Repent that e'er thy tongue,
　　Hath so betray'd thine act. Being done unknown,
　　I should have found it afterwards well done,
　　But must condemn it now: desist, and drink.

MENAS: For this, I'll never follow
　　Thy pall'd fortunes more:
　　Who seeks and will not take, when once 'tis offer'd,
　　Shall never find it more.

POMPEY: This health to Lepidus.

ANTONY: Bear him ashore,
　　I 'll pledge it for him Pompey.

ENOBARBUS: Here's to thee Menas.

MENAS: Enobarbus, welcome.

POMPEY: Fill till the cup be hid.

ENOBARBUS: There 's a strong fellow Menas.

MENAS: Why?

ENOBARBUS: A' bears the third part of the world man:
　　see'st not?

MENAS: The third part, then he is drunk: would it were all, that it might go on wheels.

ENOBARBUS: Drink thou: increase the reels.

MENAS: Come.

POMPEY: This is not yet an Alexandrian feast.

ANTONY: It ripens towards it: strike the vessels hoa,
Here's to Cæsar.

CÆSAR: I could well forbear 't. It's monstrous labour when I wash my brain, and it grow fouler.

ANTONY: Be a child o' th' time.

CÆSAR; Possess it, I'll make answer: but I had rather fast from all, four days, than drink so much in one.

ENOBARBUS: Ha my brave Emperor, shall we dance now the Egyptian Bacchanals, and celebrate our drink?

POMPEY: Let 's ha 't good soldier.

ANTONY: Come, let's all take hands,
Till that the conquering wine hath steep'd our sense,
In soft and delicate Lethe.

ENOBARBUS: All take hands:
Make battery to our ears with the loud music,
The while, I'll place you, then the boy shall sing.
The holding every man shall bear 't as loud,
As his strong sides can volley.

Music plays. Enobarbus places them hand in hand.

THE SONG

Come thou Monarch of the Vine,
Plumpy Bacchus, with pink eyne:
In thy fats our cares be drown'd,
With thy grapes our hairs be crown'd.
Cup us till the world go round,
Cup us till the world go round.

CÆSAR: What would you more?
  Pompey good night. Good brother
  Let me request you of our graver business
  Frowns at this levity. Gentle Lords let's part,
  You see we have burnt our cheeks. Strong Enobarb
  Is weaker than the wine, and mine own tongue
  Splits what it speaks: the wild disguise hath almost
  Antick'd us all. What needs more words? Good night.
  Good Antony your hand.
POMPEY: I'll try you on the shore.
ANTONY: And shall Sir, give 's your hand.
POMPEY: Oh Antony, you have my father's house.
  But what, we are friends?
  Come down into the boat.
ENOBARBUS: Take heed you fall not Menas: I'll not on
    shore,
  No to my cabin: these drums,
  These trumpets, flutes: what
  Let Neptune hear, we bid a loud farewell
  To these great fellows. Sound and be hang'd, sound out.

Sound a flourish with drums.

ENOBARBUS: Hoo says a' there 's my cap.
MENAS: Hoa, noble Captain, come.

Exeunt.

III. I

*Enter Ventidius as it were in triumph, with Silius, the
dead body of Pacorus borne before him.*

VENTIDIUS: Now darting Parthia art thou struck, and now
  Pleas'd Fortune does of Marcus Crassus' death
  Make me revenger. Bear the King's son's body,

Before our army: thy Pacorus, Orodes,
Pays this for Marcus Crassus.
SILIUS: Noble Ventidius,
  Whilst yet with Parthian blood thy sword is warm,
  The fugitive Parthians follow. Spur through Media,
  Mesopotamia, and the shelters, whither
  The routed fly. So thy grand Captain Antony
  Shall set thee on triumphant chariots, and
  Put garlands on thy head.
VENTIDIUS: Oh Silius, Silius,
  I have done enough. A lower place note well
  May make too great an act. For learn this Silius,
  Better to leave undone, than by our deed
  Acquire too high a fame, when him we serve 's away.
  Cæsar and Antony, have ever won
  More in their officer, than person. Sossius
  One of my place in Syria, his Lieutenant,
  For quick accumulation of renown,
  Which he achiev'd by th' minute, lost his favour.
  Who does i' th' wars more than his Captain can,
  Becomes his Captain's Captain: and ambition
  (The soldier's virtue) rather makes choice of loss
  Than gain, which darkens him.
  I could do more to do Antonius good,
  But 'twould offend him. And in his offence,
  Should my performance perish.
SILIUS: Thou hast Ventidius that, without the which a
  soldier and his sword grants scarce distinction: thou wilt
  write to Antony?
VENTIDIUS: I'll humbly signify what in his name,
  That magical word of war we have effected,
  How with his banners, and his well paid ranks,
  The ne'er-yet beaten horse of Parthia,

We have jaded out o' th' field.

SILIUS: Where is he now?

VENTIDIUS: He purposeth to Athens, whither with what
haste
The weight we must convey with 's, will permit,
We shall appear before him. On there, pass along.

Exeunt.

III. 2

Enter Agrippa at one door, Enobarbus at another.

AGRIPPA: What are the brothers parted?

ENOBARBUS: They have dispatch'd with Pompey, he is
gone,
The other three are sealing. Octavia weeps
To part from Rome: Cæsar is sad, and Lepidus
Since Pompey's feast, as Menas says, is troubled
With the green sickness.

AGRIPPA: 'Tis a noble Lepidus.

ENOBARBUS: A very fine one: oh, how he loves Cæsar.

AGRIPPA: Nay but how dearly he adores Mark Antony.

ENOBARBUS: Cæsar? Why he's the Jupiter of men.

AGRIPPA: What's Antony, the God of Jupiter?

ENOBARBUS: Spake you of Cæsar? How, the nonpareil?

AGRIPPA: Oh Antony, oh thou Arabian bird!

ENOBARBUS: Would you praise Cæsar, say Cæsar! go
no further.

AGRIPPA: Indeed he plied them both with excellent praises.

ENOBARBUS: But he loves Cæsar best, yet he loves An-
tony:
Hoo, hearts, tongues, figure,
Scribes, bards, poets, cannot
Think, speak, cast, write, sing, number: hoo,

His love to Antony. But as for Cæsar,
Kneel down, kneel down and wonder.

AGRIPPA: Both he loves.

ENOBARBUS: They are his shards, and he their beetle, so:
This is to horse: adieu, noble Agrippa.

AGRIPPA: Good fortune worthy soldier, and farewell.

Enter Cæsar, Antony, Lepidus, and Octavia.

ANTONY: No further Sir.

CÆSAR: You take from me a great part of myself:
Use me well in 't. Sister, prove such a wife
As my thoughts make thee, and as my farthest band
Shall pass on thy approof: most noble Antony,
Let not the piece of virtue which is set
Betwixt us, as the cement of our love
To keep it builded, be the ram to batter
The fortress of it: for better might we
Have lov'd without this mean, if on both parts
This be not cherish'd.

ANTONY: Make me not offended, in your distrust.

CÆSAR: I have said.

ANTONY: You shall not find,
Though you be therein curious, the least cause
For what you seem to fear, so the Gods keep you,
And make the hearts of Romans serve your ends:
We will here part.

CÆSAR: Farewell my dearest sister, fare thee well,
The elements be kind to thee, and make
Thy spirits all of comfort: fare thee well.

OCTAVIA: My noble brother.

ANTONY: The April's in her eyes, it is Love's spring,
And these the showers to bring it on: be cheerful.

OCTAVIA: Sir, look well to my husband's house: and—

CÆSAR: What Octavia?

OCTAVIA: I'll tell you in your ear.

ANTONY: Her tongue will not obey her heart, nor can
Her heart inform her tongue.
The swans' down feather
That stands upon the swell at the full of tide:
And neither way inclines.

ENOBARBUS: Will Cæsar weep?

AGRIPPA: He has a cloud in 's face.

ENOBARBUS: He were the worse for that were he a horse,
so is he being a man.

AGRIPPA: Why Enobarbus:
When Antony found Julius Cæsar dead,
He cried almost to roaring: and he wept,
When at Philippi he found Brutus slain.

ENOBARBUS: That year indeed, he was troubled with a
rheum,
What willingly he did confound, he wail'd,
Believe 't till I weep too.

CÆSAR: No sweet Octavia,
You shall hear from me still: the time shall not
Out-go my thinking on you.

ANTONY: Come Sir, come,
I'll wrastle with you in my strength of love,
Look here I have you, thus I let you go,
And give you to the Gods.

CÆSAR: Adieu, be happy.

LEPIDUS: Let all the number of the stars give light
To thy fair way.

CÆSAR: Farewell, farewell.

Kisses Octavia.

ANTONY: Farewell.

Trumpets sound. Exeunt.

Enter Cleopatra, Charmian, Iras, and Alexas.

CLEOPATRA: Where is the fellow?

ALEXAS: Half afear'd to come.

CLEOPATRA: Go to, go to: come hither Sir.

Enter the Messenger as before.

ALEXAS: Good Majesty: Herod of Jewry dare not look upon you, but when you are well pleas'd.

CLEOPATRA: That Herod's head, I'll have: but how? When Antony is gone, through whom I might command it: come thou near.

MESSENGER: Most gracious Majesty.

CLEOPATRA: Didst thou behold Octavia?

MESSENGER: Ay dread Queen.

CLEOPATRA: Where?

MESSENGER: Madam in Rome, I look'd her in the face: and saw her led between her brother, and Mark Antony.

CLEOPATRA: Is she as tall as me?

MESSENGER: She is not, Madam.

CLEOPATRA: Didst hear her speak? Is she shrill-tongu'd or low?

MESSENGER: Madam, I heard her speak, she is low voic'd.

CLEOPATRA: That's not so good: he cannot like her long.

CHARMIAN: Like her? Oh Isis: 'tis impossible.

CLEOPATRA: I think so Charmian: dull of tongue, and dwarfish.

What majesty is in her gait, remember
If e'er thou look'dst on majesty.

MESSENGER: She creeps: her motion, and her station are as one,

She shows a body, rather than a life,
A statue, than a breather.

CLEOPATRA: Is this certain?

MESSENGER: Or I have no observance.

CHARMIAN: Three in Egypt cannot make better note.

CLEOPATRA: He's very knowing, I do perceive 't,
There's nothing in her yet.
The fellow has good judgement.

CHARMIAN: Excellent.

CLEOPATRA: Guess at her years, I prithee.

MESSENGER: Madam, she was a widow.

CLEOPATRA: Widow? Charmian, hark.

MESSENGER: And I do think she's thirty.

CLEOPATRA: Bear'st thou her face in mind? is 't long or
round?

MESSENGER: Round, even to faultiness.

CLEOPATRA: For the most part too, they are foolish that
are so. Her hair what colour?

MESSENGER: Brown Madam: and her forehead
As low as she would wish it.

CLEOPATRA: There's gold for thee,
Thou must not take my former sharpness ill,
I will employ thee back again: I find thee
Most fit for business. Go, make thee ready,
Our letters are prepar'd.
                    Exit Messenger.

CHARMIAN: A proper man.

CLEOPATRA: Indeed he is so: I repent me much
That so I harried him. Why methinks by him,
This creature 's no such thing.

CHARMIAN: Nothing Madam.

CLEOPATRA: The man hath seen some Majesty, and should
know.

CHARMIAN: Hath he seen Majesty? Isis else defend: and
serving you so long.

CLEOPATRA: I have one thing more to ask him yet good
 Charmian: but 'tis no matter, thou shalt bring him to
 me where I will write: all may be well enough.
CHARMIAN: I warrant you Madam.

Exeunt.

III. 4

Enter Antony and Octavia.

ANTONY: Nay, nay, Octavia, not only that,
 That were excusable, that and thousands more
 Of semblable import, but he hath wag'd
 New wars 'gainst Pompey. Made his will, and read it,
 To public ear, spoke scantly of me,
 When perforce he could not
 But pay me terms of honour: cold and sickly
 He vented then most narrow measure; lent me,
 When the best hint was given him: he not look 't,
 Or did it from his teeth.
OCTAVIA: Oh my good Lord,
 Believe not all, or if you must believe,
 Stomach not all. A more unhappy Lady,
 If this division chance, ne'er stood between
 Praying for both parts:
 The good Gods will mock me presently,
 When I shall pray: Oh bless my Lord, and husband,
 Undo that prayer, by crying out as loud,
 Oh bless my brother. Husband win, win brother,
 Prays, and destroys the prayer, no midway
 'Twixt these extremes at all.
ANTONY: Gentle Octavia,
 Let your best love draw to that point which seeks
 Best to preserve it: if I lose mine honour,

I lose myself: better I were not yours
Than yours so branchless. But as you requested,
Yourself shall go between 's, the mean time Lady,
I 'll raise the preparation of a war
Shall stain your brother. Make your soonest haste.
So your desires are yours.

OCTAVIA: Thanks to my Lord,
The Jove of power make me most weak, most weak,
Your reconciler: wars 'twixt you twain would be,
As if the world should cleave, and that slain men
Should solder up the rift.

ANTONY: When it appears to you where this begins,
Turn your displeasure that way, for our faults
Can never be so equal, that your love
Can equally move with them. Provide your going,
Choose your own company, and command what cost
Your heart has mind to.

Exeunt.

III. 5

Enter Enobarbus, and Eros.

ENOBARBUS: How now friend Eros?

EROS: There 's strange news come Sir.

ENOBARBUS: What man?

EROS: Cæsar and Lepidus have made wars upon Pompey.

ENOBARBUS: This is old, what is the success?

EROS: Cæsar having made use of him in the wars 'gainst
Pompey, presently denied him rivality, would not let him
partake in the glory of the action, and not resting here,
accuses him of letters he had formerly wrote to Pompey.
Upon his own appeal seizes him, so the poor third is
up, till death enlarge his confine.

ENOBARBUS: Then would thou hast a pair of chaps no
  more, and throw between them all the food thou hast,
  they'll grind the one the other. Where 's Antony?
EROS: He 's walking in the garden thus, and spurns
  The rush that lies before him. Cries Fool Lepidus,
  And threats the throat of that his officer,
  That murder'd Pompey.
ENOBARBUS: Our great Navy 's rigg'd.
EROS: For Italy and Cæsar: more Domitius,
  My Lord desires you presently: my news
  I might have told hereafter.
ENOBARBUS: 'Twill be naught, but let it be: bring me to
  Antony.
EROS: Come Sir.

                    Exeunt.

III. 6

Enter Agrippa, Mæcenas, and Cæsar.
CÆSAR: Contemning Rome he has done all this, and more
  In Alexandria: here 's the manner of 't:
  I' th' Market-place on a tribunal silver'd,
  Cleopatra and himself in chairs of gold
  Were publicly enthron'd: at the feet, sat
  Cæsarion whom they call my father's son,
  And all the unlawful issue, that their lust
  Since then hath made between them. Unto her,
  He gave the stablishment of Egypt, made her
  Of lower Syria, Cyprus, Lydia, absolute Queen.
MÆCENAS: This in the public eye?
CÆSAR: I' th' common show-place, where they exercise,
  His sons he there proclaim'd the King of Kings,
  Great Media, Parthia, and Armenia

He gave to Alexander. To Ptolemy he assign'd,
Syria, Cilicia, and Phœnicia: she
In th' habiliments of the Goddess Isis
That day appear'd, and oft before gave audience,
As 'tis reported so.

MÆCENAS: Let Rome be thus inform'd.

AGRIPPA: Who queasy with his insolence already,
Will their good thoughts call from him.

CÆSAR: The people knows it,
And have now receiv'd his accusations.

AGRIPPA: Who does he accuse?

CÆSAR: Cæsar, and that having in Sicily,
Sextus Pompeius spoil'd, we had not rated him
His part o' th' Isle. Then does he say, he lent me
Some shipping unrestor'd. Lastly, he frets
That Lepidus of the Triumvirate, should be depos'd,
And being that, we detain all his revenue.

AGRIPPA: Sir, this should be answer'd.

CÆSAR: 'Tis done already, and the messenger gone:
I have told him Lepidus was grown too cruel,
That he his high authority abus'd,
And did deserve his change: for what I have conquer'd,
I grant him part: but then in his Armenia,
And other of his conquer'd Kingdoms, I demand the
like.

MÆCENAS: He'll never yield to that.

CÆSAR: Nor must not then be yielded to in this.

Enter Octavia with her train.

OCTAVIA: Hail Cæsar, and my Lord, hail most dear Cæsar.

CÆSAR: That ever I should call thee castaway.

OCTAVIA: You have not call'd me so, nor have you cause.

CÆSAR: Why have you stol'n upon us thus? You come not
Like Cæsar's sister. The wife of Antony

Should have an army for an usher, and
The neighs of horse to tell of her approach,
Long ere she did appear. The trees by th' way
Should have borne men, and expectation fainted,
Longing for what it had not. Nay the dust
Should have ascended to the roof of Heaven,
Rais'd by your populous troops: but you are come
A market-maid to Rome, and have prevented
The ostentation of our love: which left unshown,
Is often left unlov'd: we should have met you
By sea and land, supplying every stage
With an augmented greeting.

OCTAVIA: Good my Lord,
To come thus was I not constrain'd, but did it
On my free will. My Lord Mark Antony,
Hearing that you prepar'd for war, acquainted
My grieved ear withal: whereon I begg'd
His pardon for return.

CÆSAR: Which soon he granted,
Being an obstruct 'tween his lust, and him.

OCTAVIA: Do not say so, my Lord.

CÆSAR: I have eyes upon him,
And his affairs come to me on the wind: where is he
now?

OCTAVIA: My Lord, in Athens.

CÆSAR: No my most wronged sister, Cleopatra
Hath nodded him to her. He hath given his Empire
Up to a whore, who now are levying
The Kings o' th' earth for war. He hath assembled,
Bocchus the King of Libya, Archelaus
Of Cappadocia, Philadelphos King
Of Paphlagonia: the Thracian King Adallas,
King Malchus of Arabia, King of Pont,

Herod of Jewry, Mithridates King
Of Comagene, Polemon and Amyntas,
The Kings of Mede, and Lycaonia,
With a more larger list of sceptres.

OCTAVIA: Aye me most wretched,
That have my heart parted betwixt two friends,
That does afflict each other.

CÆSAR: Welcome hither: your letters did withhold our
breaking forth
Till we perceiv'd both how you were wrong led,
And we in negligent danger: cheer your heart,
Be you not troubled with the time, which drives
O'er your content, these strong necessities,
But let determin'd things to destiny
Hold unbewail'd their way. Welcome to Rome,
Nothing more dear to me: you are abus'd
Beyond the mark of thought: and the high Gods
To do you justice, makes his ministers
Of us, and those that love you. Best of comfort,
And ever welcome to us.

AGRIPPA: Welcome Lady.

MÆCENAS: Welcome dear Madam,
Each heart in Rome does love and pity you,
Only th' adulterous Antony, most large
In his abominations, turns you off,
And gives his potent regiment to a trull
That noises it against us.

OCTAVIA: Is it so Sir?

CÆSAR: Most certain: sister welcome: pray you
Be ever known to patience. My dear'st sister.

Exeunt.

III. 7

Enter Cleopatra, and Enobarbus.

CLEOPATRA: I will be even with thee, doubt it not.

ENOBARBUS: But why, why, why?

CLEOPATRA: Thou hast forspoke my being in these wars,
And say'st it is not fit.

ENOBARBUS: Well: is it, is it?

CLEOPATRA: If not, denounc'd against us, why should
not we be there in person?

ENOBARBUS: Well, I could reply: if we should serve with
horse and mares together, the horse were merely lost:
the mares would bear a soldier and his horse.

CLEOPATRA: What is 't you say?

ENOBARBUS: Your presence needs must puzzle Antony,
Take from his heart, take from his brain, from 's time,
What should not then be spar'd. He is already
Traduc'd for levity, and 'tis said in Rome,
That Photinus an eunuch, and your maids
Manage this war.

CLEOPATRA: Sink Rome, and their tongues rot
That speak against us. A charge we bear i' th' war,
And as the president of my Kingdom will
Appear there for a man. Speak not against it,
I will not stay behind.

Enter Antony and Canidius.

ENOBARBUS: Nay I have done, here comes the Emperor.

ANTONY: Is it not strange Canidius,
That from Tarentum, and Brundusium,
He could so quickly cut the Ionian Sea,
And take in Toryne? You have heard on 't, Sweet?

CLEOPATRA: Celerity is never more admir'd,
Than by the negligent.

ANTONY: A good rebuke,
  Which might have well becom'd the best of men
  To taunt at slackness. Canidius, we
  Will fight with him by sea.
CLEOPATRA: By sea, what else?
CANIDIUS: Why will my Lord do so?
ANTONY: For that he dares us to 't.
ENOBARBUS: So hath my Lord dar'd him to single
    fight.
CANIDIUS: Ay, and to wage this battle at Pharsalia,
  Where Cæsar fought with Pompey. But these offers
  Which serve not for his vantage, he shakes off,
  And so should you.
ENOBARBUS: Your ships are not well mann'd,
  Your mariners are muleters, reapers, people
  Ingross'd by swift impress. In Cæsar's fleet,
  Are those, that often have 'gainst Pompey fought,
  Their ships are yare, yours heavy: no disgrace
  Shall fall you for refusing him at sea,
  Being prepar'd for land.
ANTONY: By sea, by sea.
ENOBARBUS: Most worthy Sir, you therein throw away
  The absolute soldiership you have by land,
  Distract your army, which doth most consist
  Of war-mark'd footmen, leave unexecuted
  Your own renowned knowledge, quite forgo
  The way which promises assurance, and
  Give up yourself merely to chance and hazard,
  From firm security.
ANTONY: I'll fight at sea.
CLEOPATRA: I have sixty sails, Cæsar none better.
ANTONY: Our overplus of shipping will we burn,
  And with the rest full-mann'd, from th' head of Actium

Beat th' approaching Cæsar.   But if we fail,
We then can do 't at land.

Enter a Messenger.

Thy business?

MESSENGER: The news is true, my Lord, he is descried,
Cæsar has taken Toryne.

ANTONY: Can he be there in person? 'Tis impossible,
Strange, that his power should be. Canidius,
Our nineteen Legions thou shalt hold by land,
And our twelve thousand horse. We 'll to our ship,
Away my Thetis.

Enter a Soldier.

How now worthy soldier?

SOLDIER: Oh noble Emperor, do not fight by sea,
Trust not to rotten planks: do you misdoubt
This sword, and these my wounds; let th' Egyptians
And the Phœnicians go a-ducking: we
Have us'd to conquer standing on the earth,
And fighting foot by foot.

ANTONY: Well, well, away.

Exeunt Antony, Cleopatra, and Enobarbus.

SOLDIER: By Hercules I think I am i' th' right.

CANIDIUS: Soldier thou art: but his whole action grows
Not in the power on 't: so our leader 's led,
And we are women's men.

SOLDIER: You keep by land the legions and the horse
whole, do you not?

CANIDIUS: Marcus Octavius, Marcus Justeius,
Publicola, and Cælius, are for sea:
But we keep whole by land. This speed of Cæsar's
Carries beyond belief.

SOLDIER: While he was yet in Rome,
His power went out in such distractions,

As beguil'd all spies.

CANIDIUS: Who 's his Lieutenant, hear you?

SOLDIER: They say, one Taurus.

CANIDIUS: Well, I know the man.

Enter a Messenger.

MESSENGER: The Emperor calls Canidius.

CANIDIUS: With news the time's with labour,
And throes forth each minute some.

Exeunt.

III. 8

Enter Cæsar, and Taurus, with his army, marching.

CÆSAR: Taurus?

TAURUS: My Lord.

CÆSAR: Strike not by land,
Keep whole, provoke not battle
Till we have done at sea. Do not exceed
The prescript of this scroll: our fortune lies
Upon this jump.

Exeunt.

III. 9

Enter Antony, and Enobarbus.

ANTONY: Set we our squadrons on yond side o' th' hill,
In eye of Cæsar's battle from which place
We may the number of the ships behold,
And so proceed accordingly.

Exeunt.

III. 10

Canidius marcheth with his land army one way over the stage:
and Taurus the Lieutenant of Cæsar the other way.
After their going in, is heard the noise of a sea-fight.
Alarum. Enter Enobarbus.

ENOBARBUS: Naught, naught, all naught, I can behold no
    longer:
    Th' *Antoniad*, the Egyptian Admiral,
    With all their sixty fly, and turn the rudder:
    To see 't, mine eyes are blasted.
Enter Scarus.

SCARUS: Gods and Goddesses, all the whole synod of
    them!

ENOBARBUS: What 's thy passion.

SCARUS: The greater cantle of the world, is lost
    With very ignorance, we have kiss'd away
    Kingdoms, and Provinces.

ENOBARBUS: How appears the fight?

SCARUS: On our side, like the token'd pestilence,
    Where death is sure. Yon ribaudred nag of Egypt,
    (Whom leprosy o'ertake) i' th' midst o' th' fight.
    When vantage, like a pair of twins appear'd
    Both as the same, or rather ours the elder;
    (The breeze upon her) like a cow in June,
    Hoists sails, and flies.

ENOBARBUS: That I beheld:
    Mine eyes did sicken at the sight, and could not
    Endure a further view.

SCARUS: She once being loof'd,
    The noble ruin of her magic, Antony,
    Claps on his sea-wing, and (like a doting mallard)
    Leaving the fight in heighth, flies after her:

I never saw an action of such shame;
Experience, manhood, honour, ne'er before,
Did violate so itself.

ENOBARBUS: Alack, alack.

Enter Canidius.

CANIDIUS: Our fortune on the sea is out of breath,
And sinks most lamentably. Had our General
Been what he knew himself, it had gone well:
Oh he has given example for our flight,
Most grossly by his own.

ENOBARBUS: Ay, are you thereabouts? Why then good
night indeed.

CANIDIUS: Toward Peloponnesus are they fled.

SCARUS: 'Tis easy to 't,
And there I will attend what further comes,

CANIDIUS: To Cæsar will I render
My Legions and my horse, six Kings already
Show me the way of yielding.

ENOBARBUS: I'll yet follow
The wounded chance of Antony, though my reason
Sits in the wind against me.

Exeunt.

III. 11

Enter Antony with Attendants.

ANTONY: Hark, the land bids me tread no more upon 't,
It is asham'd to bear me. Friends, come hither,
I am so lated in the world, that I
Have lost my way for ever. I have a ship,
Laden with gold, take that, divide it: fly,
And make your peace with Cæsar.

ALL: Fly? Not we.

ANTONY: I have fled myself, and have instructed cowards
  To run, and show their shoulders. Friends be gone,
  I have myself resolv'd upon a course,
  Which has no need of you. Be gone,
  My treasure's in the harbour. Take it: oh,
  I follow'd that I blush to look upon,
  My very hairs do mutiny: for the white
  Reprove the brown for rashness, and they them
  For fear, and doting. Friends be gone, you shall
  Have letters from me to some friends, that will
  Sweep your way for you. Pray you look not sad,
  Nor make replies of loathness, take the hint
  Which my despair proclaims. Let that be left
  Which leaves itself: to the sea-side straightway;
  I will possess you of that ship and treasure.
  Leave me, I pray a little: pray you now,
  Nay do so: for indeed I have lost command,
  Therefore I pray you, I'll see you by and by.

                  Sits down.

    Enter Cleopatra led by Charmian, Iras and Eros.

EROS: Nay gentle Madam, to him, comfort him.

IRAS: Do most dear Queen.

CHARMIAN: Do, why, what else?

CLEOPATRA: Let me sit down: Oh Juno.

ANTONY: No, no, no, no, no.

EROS: See you here, Sir?

ANTONY: Oh fie, fie, fie.

CHARMIAN: Madam.

IRAS: Madam, oh good Empress.

EROS: Sir, sir.

ANTONY: Yes my Lord, yes; he at Philippi kept
  His sword e'en like a dancer, while I struck
  The lean and wrinkled Cassius, and 'twas I

That the mad Brutus ended: he alone
Dealt on lieutenantry, and no practice had
In the brace squares of war: yet now: no matter.

CLEOPATRA: Ah stand by.

EROS: The Queen my Lord, the Queen.

IRAS: Go to him, Madam, speak to him,
He is unqualitied with very shame.

CLEOPATRA: Well then, sustain me: Oh.

EROS: Most noble Sir arise, the Queen approaches,
Her head 's declin'd, and death will seize her, but
Your comfort makes the rescue.

ANTONY: I have offended reputation,
A most unnoble swerving.

EROS: Sir, the Queen.

ANTONY: Oh whither has thou led me Egypt, see
How I convey my shame, out of thine eyes,
By looking back what I have left behind
Stroy'd in dishonour.

CLEOPATRA: Oh my Lord, my Lord,
Forgive my fearful sails, I little thought
You would have followed.

ANTONY: Egypt, thou knew'st too well,
My heart was to thy rudder tied by th' strings,
And thou should'st stow me after. O'er my spirit
The full supremacy thou knew'st, and that
Thy beck, might from the bidding of the Gods
Command me.

CLEOPATRA: Oh my pardon.

ANTONY: Now I must
To the young man send humble treaties, dodge
And palter in the shifts of lowness, who
With half the bulk o' th' world play'd as I pleas'd,
Making and marring fortunes. You did know

How much you were my conqueror, and that
My sword, made weak by my affection, would
Obey it on all cause.

CLEOPATRA: Pardon, pardon.

ANTONY: Fall not a tear I say, one of them rates
All that is won and lost: give me a kiss,
Even this repays me.
We sent our schoolmaster, is a' come back?
Love I am full of lead: some wine
Within there, and our viands: Fortune knows,
We scorn her most, when most she offers blows.

Exeunt.

III. 12

Enter Cæsar, Agrippa, Dolabella, and Thidias,
with others.

CÆSAR: Let him appear that 's come from Antony.
Know you him?

DOLABELLA: Cæsar, 'tis his schoolmaster,
An argument that he is pluck'd, when hither
He sends so poor a pinion of his wing,
Which had superfluous Kings for messengers,
Not many moons gone by.

Enter Ambassador from Antony.

CÆSAR: Approach and speak.

AMBASSADOR: Such as I am, I come from Antony:
I was of late as petty to his ends,
As is the morn-dew on the myrtle-leaf
To his grand sea.

CÆSAR: Be 't so, declare thine office.

AMBASSADOR: Lord of his fortunes he salutes thee, and
Requires to live in Egypt, which not granted

He lessens his requests, and to thee sues
To let him breathe between the Heavens and Earth
A private man in Athens: this for him.
Next Cleopatra does confess thy greatness,
Submits her to thy might, and of thee craves
The circle of the Ptolemies for her heirs,
Now hazarded to thy Grace.

CÆSAR: For Antony,
I have no ears to his request. The Queen,
Of audience, nor desire shall fail, so she
From Egypt drive her all-disgraced friend,
Or take his life there. This if she perform,
She shall not sue unheard. So to them both.

AMBASSADOR: Fortune pursue thee.

CÆSAR: Bring him through the bands:

Exit Ambassador.

To try thy eloquence, now 'tis time, dispatch,
From Antony win Cleopatra, promise
And in our name, what she requires, add more
From thine invention, offers. Women are not
In their best fortunes strong; but want will perjure
The ne'er-touch'd vestal. Try thy cunning Thidias,
Make thine own edict for thy pains, which we
Will answer as a law.

THIDIAS: Cæsar, I go.

CÆSAR: Observe how Antony becomes his flaw,
And what thou think'st his very action speaks
In every power that moves.

THIDIAS: Cæsar, I shall.

Exeunt.

III. 13

Enter Cleopatra, Enobarbus, Charmian, and Iras.

CLEOPATRA: What shall we do, Enobarbus?

ENOBARBUS: Think, and die.

CLEOPATRA: Is Antony, or we in fault for this?

ENOBARBUS: Antony only, that would make his will
   Lord of his reason. What though you fled,
   From that great face of war, whose several ranges
   Frighted each other? Why should he follow?
   The itch of his affection should not then
   Have nick'd his captainship, at such a point,
   When half to half the world oppos'd, he being
   The meered question? 'Twas a shame no less
   Than was his loss, to course your flying flags,
   And leave his navy gazing.

CLEOPATRA: Prithee peace.

Enter the Ambassador, with Antony.

ANTONY: Is that his answer?

AMBASSADOR: Ay my Lord.

ANTONY: The Queen shall then have courtesy,
   So she will yield us up.

AMBASSADOR: He says so.

ANTONY: Let her know 't.
   To the boy Cæsar send this grizzled head,
   And he will fill thy wishes to the brim,
   With Principalities.

CLEOPATRA: That head my Lord?

ANTONY: To him again, tell him he wears the rose
   Of youth upon him: from which, the world should note
   Something particular: his coin, ships, legions,
   May be a coward's, whose ministers would prevail
   Under the service of a child, as soon

As i' th' command of Cæsar. I dare him therefore
To lay his gay comparisons apart,
And answer me declin'd, sword against sword,
Ourselves alone: I'll write it: follow me.

Exeunt Antony and Ambassador.

ENOBARBUS: Yes like enough: high-battl'd Cæsar will
Unstate his happiness, and be stag'd to th' show
Against a sworder. I see men's judgements are
A parcel of their fortunes, and things outward
Do draw the inward quality after them
To suffer all alike, that he should dream,
Knowing all measures, the full Cæsar will
Answer his emptiness: Cæsar thou hast subdu'd
His judgement too.

Enter a Servant.

SERVANT: A messenger from Cæsar.

CLEOPATRA: What no more ceremony? See my women,
Against the blown rose may they stop their nose,
That kneel'd unto the buds. Admit him sir.

ENOBARBUS: Mine honesty, and I, begin to square.
The loyalty well held to fools, does make
Our faith mere folly: yet he that can endure
To follow with allegiance a fall'n Lord,
Does conquer him that did his Master conquer,
And earns a place i' th' story.

Enter Thidias.

CLEOPATRA: Cæsar's will.

THIDIAS: Hear it apart.

CLEOPATRA: None but friends: say boldly.

THIDIAS: So haply are they friends to Antony.

ENOBARBUS: He needs as many, Sir, as Cæsar has,
Or needs not us. If Cæsar please, our Master

Will leap to be his friend: for us you know,
Whose he is, we are, and that is Cæsar's.

THIDIAS: So. Thus then thou most renown'd, Cæsar en-
treats,
Not to consider in what case thou stand'st
Further than he is Cæsar.

CLEOPATRA: Go on, right royal.

THIDIAS: He knows that you embrace not Antony
As you did love, but as you fear'd him.

CLEOPATRA: Oh.

THIDIAS: The scars upon your honour, therefore he
Does pity, as constrained blemishes,
Not as deserved.

CLEOPATRA: He is a God,
And knows what is most right. Mine honour
Was not yielded, but conquer'd merely.

ENOBARBUS: To be sure of that, I will ask Antony.
Sir, sir, thou art so leaky
That we must leave thee to thy sinking, for
Thy dearest quit thee.

Exit Enobarbus.

THIDIAS: Shall I say to Cæsar,
What you require of him: for he partly begs
To be desir'd to give. It much would please him,
That of his fortunes you should make a staff
To lean upon. But it would warm his spirits
To hear from me you had left Antony,
And put yourself under his shrowd,
The universal landlord.

CLEOPATRA: What's your name?

THIDIAS: My name is Thidias.

CLEOPATRA: Most kind messenger,
Say to great Cæsar this in deputation,

I kiss his conquering hand: tell him, I am prompt
To lay my Crown at 's feet, and there to kneel.
Tell him, from his all-obeying breath, I hear
The doom of Egypt.

THIDIAS: 'Tis your noblest course:
Wisdom and Fortune combating together,
If that the former dare but what it can,
No chance may shake it. Give me grace to lay
My duty on your hand.

CLEOPATRA: Your Cæsar's father oft,
(When he hath mus'd of taking kingdoms in)
Bestow'd his lips on that unworthy place,
As it rain'd kisses.

Enter Antony and Enobarbus.

ANTONY: Favours? By Jove that thunders. What art thou
fellow?

THIDIAS: One that but performs
The bidding of the fullest man, and worthiest
To have command obey'd.

ENOBARBUS: You will be whipp'd.

ANTONY: Approach there: ah you kite. Now Gods and
devils,
Authority melts from me of late. When I cried hoa,
Like boys unto a muss, Kings would start forth,
And cry, your will. Have you no ears?
I am Antony yet. Take hence this Jack, and whip him.
Enter a Servant.

ENOBARBUS: 'Tis better playing with a lion's whelp,
Than with an old one dying.

ANTONY: Moon and stars,
Whip him: were 't twenty of the greatest Tributaries
That do acknowledge Cæsar, should I find them

So saucy with the hand of she here, what's her name
Since she was Cleopatra? Whip him fellows,
Till like a boy you see him cringe his face,
And whine aloud for mercy. Take him hence.

THIDIAS: Mark Antony.

ANTONY: Tug him away: being whipp'd
Bring him again, the Jack of Cæsar's shall
Bear us an errand to him.

Exeunt with Thidias.

You were half blasted ere I knew you: ha?
Have I my pillow left unpress'd in Rome,
Forborne the getting of a lawful race,
And by a gem of women, to be abus'd
By one that looks on feeders?

CLEOPATRA: Good my Lord.

ANTONY: You have been a boggler ever,
But when we in our viciousness grow hard
(Oh misery on 't) the wise Gods seel our eyes
In our own filth, drop our clear judgements, make us
Adore our errors, laugh at 's while we strut
To our confusion.

CLEOPATRA: Oh, is 't come to this?

ANTONY: I found you as a morsel, cold upon
Dead Cæsar's trencher: nay, you were a fragment
Of Cneius Pompey's, besides what hotter hours
Unregister'd in vulgar fame, you have
Luxuriously pick'd out. For I am sure,
Though you can guess what temperance should be,
You know not what it is.

CLEOPATRA: Wherefore is this?

ANTONY: To let a fellow that will take rewards,
And say, God quit you, be familiar with
My playfellow, your hand; this kingly seal,

And plighter of high hearts. O that I were
Upon the hill of Basan, to outroar
The horned herd, for I have savage cause,
And to proclaim it civilly, were like
A halter'd neck, which does the hangman thank,
For being yare about him. Is he whipp'd?

Enter a Servant with Thidias.

SERVANT: Soundly, my Lord.
ANTONY: Cried he? and begg'd a' pardon?
SERVANT: He did ask favour.
ANTONY: If that thy father live, let him repent
Thou wast not made his daughter, and be thou sorry
To follow Cæsar in his triumph, since
Thou hast been whipp'd for following him. Henceforth
The white hand of a lady fever thee,
Shake thou to look on 't. Get thee back to Cæsar,
Tell him thy entertainment: look thou say
He makes me angry with him. For he seems
Proud and disdainful, harping on what I am,
Not what he knew I was. He makes me angry,
And at this time most easy 'tis to do 't:
When my good stars, that were my former guides
Have empty left their orbs, and shot their fires
Into th' abysm of hell. If he mislike
My speech, and what is done, tell him he has
Hipparchus, my enfranched bondman, whom
He may at pleasure whip, or hang, or torture,
As he shall like to quit me. Urge it thou:
Hence with thy stripes, begone.

Exit Thidias.

CLEOPATRA: Have you done yet?
ANTONY: Alack our terrene Moon is now eclips'd,
And it portends alone the fall of Antony.

CLEOPATRA: I must stay his time?

ANTONY: To flatter Cæsar, would you mingle eyes
  With one that ties his points?

CLEOPATRA: Not know me yet?

ANTONY: Cold-hearted toward me?

CLEOPATRA: Ah, dear, if I be so,
  From my cold heart let Heaven engender hail,
  And poison it in the source, and the first stone
  Drop in my neck: as it determines so
  Dissolve my life, the next Cæsarion smite,
  Till by degrees the memory of my womb,
  Together with my brave Egyptians all,
  By the discandering of this pelleted storm,
  Lie graveless, till the flies and gnats of Nile
  Have buried them for prey.

ANTONY: I am satisfied:
  Cæsar sits down in Alexandria, where
  I will oppose his fate. Our force by land,
  Hath nobly held, our sever'd Navy too
  Have knit again, and fleet, threatening most sea-like.
  Where hast thou been my heart? Dost thou hear Lady?
  If from the field I shall return once more
  To kiss these lips, I will appear in blood,
  I, and my sword, will earn our Chronicle,
  There's hope in 't yet.

CLEOPATRA: That's my brave Lord.

ANTONY: I will be treble-sinew'd, hearted, breath'd,
  And fight maliciously: for when mine hours
  Were nice and lucky, men did ransom lives
  Of me for jests: but now, I'll set my teeth,
  And send to darkness all that stop me. Come,
  Let's have one other gawdy night: call to me
  All my sad Captains, fill our bowls once more:

Let's mock the midnight bell.

CLEOPATRA: It is my birth-day,
I had thought t' have held it poor. But since my Lord
Is Antony again, I will be Cleopatra.

ANTONY: We will yet do well.

CLEOPATRA: Call all his noble Captains to my Lord.

ANTONY: Do so, we 'll speak to them,
And to-night I'll force
The wine peep through their scars.
Come on, my Queen,
There 's sap in 't yet. The next time I do fight
I 'll make death love me: for I will contend
Even with his pestilent scythe.

Exeunt.

ENOBARBUS: Now he 'll outstare the lightning: to be furious
Is to be frighted out of fear, and in that mood
The dove will peck the estridge; and I see still
A diminution in our Captain's brain,
Restores his heart; when valour preys in reason,
It eats the sword it fights with: I will seek
Some way to leave him.

Exit.

IV. 1

*Enter Cæsar, Agrippa, and Mæcenas with his army,
Cæsar reading a letter.*

CÆSAR: He calls me Boy, and chides as he had power
To beat me out of Egypt. My messenger
He hath whipp'd with rods, dares me to personal combat.
Cæsar to Antony: let the old ruffian know,

I have many other ways to die: meantime
Laugh at his challenge.
MÆCENAS: Cæsar must think,
When one so great begins to rage, he 's hunted
Even to falling. Give him no breath, but now
Make boot of his distraction: never anger
Made good guard for itself.
CÆSAR: Let our best heads know,
That to-morrow, the last of many battles
We mean to fight. Within our files there are,
Of those that serv'd Mark Antony but late,
Enough to fetch him in. See it done,
And feast the Army, we have store to do 't,
And they have earn'd the waste. Poor Antony.

Exeunt.

IV. 2

Enter Antony, Cleopatra, Enobarbus, Charmian, Iras,
Alexas, with others.

ANTONY: He will not fight with me, Domitius?
ENOBARBUS: No.
ANTONY: Why should he not?
ENOBARBUS: He thinks, being twenty times of better
    fortune,
He is twenty men to one.
ANTONY: To-morrow soldier,
By sea and land I 'll fight: or I will live,
Or bathe my dying honour in the blood
Shall make it live again. Woo't thou fight well.
ENOBARBUS: I'll strike, and cry, Take all.
ANTONY: Well said, come on:
Call forth my household servants, let 's to-night

Be bounteous at our meal. Give me thy hand,
>*Enter three or four Servitors.*
Thou hast been rightly honest, so hast thou,
Thou, and thou, and thou: you have serv'd me well,
And Kings have been your fellows.

CLEOPATRA: What means this?

ENOBARBUS: 'Tis one of those odd tricks which sorrow shoots
Out of the mind.

ANTONY: And thou art honest too:
I wish I could be made so many men,
And all of you clapp'd up together, in
An Antony: that I might do you service,
So good as you have done.

ALL: The Gods forbid.

ANTONY: Well, my good fellows, wait on me to-night:
Scant not my cups, and make as much of me,
As when mine Empire was your fellow too,
And suffer'd my command.

CLEOPATRA: What does he mean?

ENOBARBUS: To make his followers weep.

ANTONY: Tend me to-night;
May be, it is the period of your duty,
Haply you shall not see me more, or if,
A mangled shadow. Perchance to-morrow,
You'll serve another Master. I look on you,
As one that takes his leave. Mine honest friends,
I turn you not away, but like a Master
Married to your good service, stay till death:
Tend me to-night two hours, I ask no more,
And the Gods yield you for 't.

ENOBARBUS: What mean you, Sir,
To give them this discomfort? Look they weep,

And I an ass, am onion-ey'd; for shame,
Transform us not to women.
ANTONY: Ho, ho, ho:
 Now the witch take me, if I meant it thus.
 Grace grow where those drops fall, my hearty friends,
 You take me in too dolorous a sense,
 For I spake to you for your comfort, did desire you
 To burn this night with torches: know, my hearts,
 I hope well of to-morrow, and will lead you,
 Where rather I 'll expect victorious life,
 Than death, and honour. Let 's to supper, come,
 And drown consideration.
       Exeunt.

IV. 3

Enter a company of Soldiers.

1 SOLDIER: Brother, good night: to-morrow is the day.
2 SOLDIER: It will determine one way: fare you well.
 Heard you of nothing strange about the streets?
1 SOLDIER: Nothing: what news?
2 SOLDIER: Belike 'tis but a rumour, good night to
 you.
1 SOLDIER: Well sir, good night.
     They meet other Soldiers.
2 SOLDIER: Soldiers, have careful watch.
1 SOLDIER: And you: good night, good night.
   They place themselves in every corner of the stage.
2 SOLDIER: Here we: and if to-morrow
 Our Navy thrive, I have an absolute hope
 Our landmen will stand up.
1 SOLDIER: 'Tis a brave army, and full of purpose.
   Music of the hoboys is under the stage.

2 SOLDIER: Peace, what noise?

1 SOLDIER: List, list.

2 SOLDIER: Hark.

1 SOLDIER: Music i' th' air.

3 SOLDIER: Under the earth.

4 SOLDIER: It signs well, does it not?

3 SOLDIER: No.

1 SOLDIER: Peace I say: what should this mean?

2 SOLDIER: 'Tis the God Hercules, whom Antony loved,
Now leaves him.

1 SOLDIER: Walk, let's see if other watchmen
Do hear what we do.

2 SOLDIER: How now masters?

Speak together.

ALL: How now? how now? do you hear this?

1 SOLDIER: Ay, is 't not strange?

3 SOLDIER: Do you hear masters? Do you hear?

1 SOLDIER: Follow the noise so far as we have quarter.
Let's see how it will give off.

ALL: Content: 'tis strange.

Exeunt.

IV.4

Enter Antony and Cleopatra, with others.

ANTONY: Eros, mine armour Eros.

CLEOPATRA: Sleep a little.

ANTONY: No my chuck. Eros, come mine armour, Eros.

Enter Eros.

Come good fellow, put mine iron on,
If Fortune be not ours to-day, it is
Because we brave her. Come.

CLEOPATRA: Nay, I 'll help too, Antony.
　What 's this for?
ANTONY: Ah let be, let be, thou art
　The armourer of my heart: false, false, this, this.
CLEOPATRA: Sooth la I 'll help: thus it must be.
ANTONY: Well, well, we shall thrive now.
　Seest thou my good fellow. Go, put on thy defences.
EROS: Briefly Sir.
CLEOPATRA: Is not this buckled well?
ANTONY: Rarely, rarely:
　He that unbuckles this, till we do please
　To daff't for our repose, shall hear a storm.
　Thou fumblest Eros, and my Queen's a squire
　More tight at this, than thou: dispatch. O Love,
　That thou couldst see my wars to-day, and knew'st
　The royal occupation, thou shouldst see
　A workman in 't.

Enter an armed Soldier.

　Good morrow to thee, welcome,
　Thou look'st like him that knows a warlike charge:
　To business that we love, we rise betime,
　And go to 't with delight.
SOLDIER: A thousand Sir, early though 't be, have on their
　Riveted trim, and at the port expect you.

Shout. Trumpets flourish.

Enter Captains, and Soldiers.

ALEXAS: The morn is fair: good morrow General.
ALL: Good morrow General.
ANTONY: 'Tis well blown lads.
　This morning, like the spirit of a youth
　That means to be of note, begins betimes.
　So, so: come give me that, this way, well said.

Fare thee well Dame, whate'er becomes of me,
This is a soldier's kiss: rebukeable,
And worthy shameful check it were, to stand
On more mechanic compliment, I'll leave thee.
Now like a man of steel, you that will fight,
Follow me close, I 'll bring you to 't: adieu.

Exeunt.

CHARMIAN: Please you retire to your chamber?
CLEOPATRA: Lead me:
He goes forth gallantly: that he and Cæsar might
Determine this great war in single fight;
Then Antony; but now. Well on.

Exeunt.

IV.5

Trumpets sound. Enter Antony, Eros and a Soldier.

EROS: The Gods make this a happy day to Antony.
ANTONY: Would thou, and those thy scars had once prevail'd
To make me fight at land.
EROS: Hadst thou done so,
The Kings that have revolted, and the soldier
That has this morning left thee, would have still
Follow'd thy heels.
ANTONY: Who 's gone this morning?
EROS: Who? one ever near thee, call for Enobarbus,
He shall not hear thee, or from Cæsar's camp,
Say I am none of thine.
ANTONY: What sayest thou?
SOLDIER: Sir he is with Cæsar.
EROS: Sir, his chests and treasure he has not with him.
ANTONY: Is he gone?

SOLDIER: Most certain.

ANTONY: Go Eros, send his treasure after, do it,
 Detain no jot I charge thee: write to him,
 (I will subscribe) gentle adieus, and greetings;
 Say, that I wish he never find more cause
 To change a Master. Oh my fortunes have
 Corrupted honest men. Dispatch: Enobarbus.
 Exeunt.

IV.6

*Flourish. Enter Agrippa, Cæsar, with Enobarbus,
 and Dolabella.*

CÆSAR. Go forth Agrippa, and begin the fight:
 Our will is Antony be took alive;
 Make it so known.

AGRIPPA: Cæsar, I shall.
 Exit.

CÆSAR: The time of universal peace is near:
 Prove this a prosp'rous day, the three-nook'd world
 Shall bear the olive freely.
 Enter a Messenger.

MESSENGER: Antony is come into the field.

CÆSAR: Go charge Agrippa,
 Plant those that have revolted in the vant,
 That Antony may seem to spend his fury
 Upon himself.
 Exeunt. Manet Enobarbus.

ENOBARBUS: Alexas did revolt, and went to Jewry on
 Affairs of Antony, there did dissuade
 Great Herod to incline himself to Cæsar,
 And leave his Master Antony. For this pains,
 Cæsar hath hang'd him: Canidius and the rest

That fell away, have entertainment but
No honourable trust: I have done ill,
Of which I do accuse myself so sorely,
That I will joy no more.

Enter a Soldier of Cæsar's.

SOLDIER: Enobarbus, Antony
Hath after thee sent all thy treasure, with
His bounty overplus. The messenger
Came on my guard, and at thy tent is now
Unloading of his mules.

ENOBARBUS: I give it you.

SOLDIER: Mock not Enobarbus,
I tell you true: best you saf'd the bringer
Out of the host, I must attend mine office,
Or would have done 't myself. Your Emperor
Continues still a Jove.

Exit.

ENOBARBUS: I am alone the villain of the earth,
And feel I am so most. Oh Antony,
Thou mine of bounty, how wouldst thou have paid
My better service, when my turpitude
Thou dost so crown with gold. This blows my heart,
If swift thought break it not: a swifter mean
Shall outstrike thought: but thought will do 't. I feel
I fight against thee: no I will go seek
Some ditch, wherein to die: the foul'st best fits
My latter part of life.

Exit.

IV.7

Alarum. Drums and trumpets.
Enter Agrippa.

AGRIPPA: Retire, we have engag'd ourselves too far:
Cæsar himself has work, and our oppression
Exceeds what we expected.

Exit.
Alarums.
Enter Antony, and Scarus wounded.

SCARUS: O my brave Emperor, this is fought indeed,
Had we done so at first, we had droven them home
With clouts about their heads.

Alarum afar off.

ANTONY: Thou bleed'st apace.

SCARUS: I had a wound here that was like a T,
But now 'tis made an H.

ANTONY: They do retire.

SCARUS: We 'll beat 'em into bench-holes, I have yet
Room for six scotches more.

Enter Eros.

EROS: They are beaten Sir, and our advantage serves
For a fair victory.

SCARUS: Let us score their backs,
And snatch 'em up, as we take hares behind,
'Tis sport to maul a runner.

ANTONY: I will reward thee
Once for thy spritely comfort, and ten-fold
For thy good valour. Come thee on.

SCARUS: I 'll halt after.

Exeunt.

Alarum. Enter Antony again in a march. Scarus,
with others.

ANTONY: We have beat him to his camp: run one before,
And let the Queen know of our guests: to-morrow
Before the sun shall see 's, we 'll spill the blood
That has to-day escap'd. I thank you all,
For doughty-handed are you, and have fought
Not as you serv'd the cause, but as 't had been
Each man 's like mine: you have shown all Hectors.
Enter the City, clip your wives, your friends,
Tell them your feats, whilst they with joyful tears
Wash the congealment from your wounds, and kiss
The honour'd gashes whole.
Enter Cleopatra.
Give me thy hand,
To this great Fairy, I 'll commend thy acts,
Make her thanks bless thee. Oh thou day o' th' world,
Chain mine arm'd neck, leap thou, attire and all
Through proof of harness to my heart, and there
Ride on the pants triumphing.
CLEOPATRA: Lord of Lords,
Oh infinite virtue, com'st thou smiling from
The world's great snare uncaught.
ANTONY: Mine nightingale,
We have beat them to their beds.
What girl, though grey
Do something mingle with our younger brown, yet ha'
we
A brain that nourishes our nerves, and can
Get goal for goal of youth. Behold this man,
Commend unto his lips thy favouring hand,

Kiss it my warrior: he hath fought to-day,
As if a God in hate of mankind, had
Destroyed in such a shape
CLEOPATRA: I 'll give thee friend.
An armour all of gold: it was a King's.
ANTONY: He has deserv'd it, were it carbuncled
Like holy Phœbus' car. Give me thy hand,
Through Alexandria make a jolly march,
Bear our hack'd targets, like the men that owe them.
Had our great Palace the capacity
To camp this host, we all would sup together,
And drink carouses to the next day's fate
Which promises royal peril. Trumpeters
With brazen din blast you the City's ear,
Make mingle with our rattling tabourines,
That heaven and earth may strike their sounds together,
Applauding our approach.
                              Exeunt.

IV.9

Enter a Centery, and his company, Enobarbus follows.
CENTERY: If we be not reliev'd within this hour,
We must return to th' court of guard: the night
Is shiny, and they say, we shall embattle
By th' second hour i' th' morn.
1 WATCH: This last day was a shrewd one to 's.
ENOBARBUS: Oh bear me witness, night.
2 WATCH: What man is this?
1 WATCH: Stand close, and list him.
ENOBARBUS: Be witness to me (O thou blessed Moon)
When men revolted shall upon record
Bear hateful memory: poor Enobarbus did

Before thy face repent.

CENTERY: Enobarbus?

2 WATCH: Peace: hark further.

ENOBARBUS: Oh sovereign Mistress of true melancholy,
The poisonous damp of night disponge upon me,
That life, a very rebel to my will,
May hang no longer on me. Throw my heart
Against the flint and hardness of my fault
Which being dried with grief, will break to powder,
And finish all foul thoughts. Oh Antony,
Nobler than my revolt is infamous,
Forgive me in thine own particular,
But let the world rank me in register
A master-leaver, and a fugitive:
Oh Antony! Oh Antony!

1 WATCH: Let 's speak to him.

CENTERY: Let 's hear him, for the things he speaks
May concern Cæsar.

2 WATCH: Let 's do so; but he sleeps.

CENTERY: Swoons rather, for so bad a prayer as his
Was never yet for sleep.

1 WATCH: Go we to him.

2 WATCH: Awake sir, awake, speak to us.

1 WATCH: Hear you sir?

CENTERY: The hand of death hath raught him.

Drums afar off.

Hark the drums demurely wake the sleepers:
Let us bear him to th' court of guard: he is of note:
Our hour is fully out.

2 WATCH: Come on then, he may recover yet.

Exeunt.

IV. 10

Enter Antony and Scarus, with their army.

ANTONY: Their preparation is to-day by sea,
  We please them not by land.
SCARUS: For both, my Lord.
ANTONY: I would they 'ld fight i' th' fire, or i' th' air,
  We 'ld fight there too. But this it is, our foot
  Upon the hills adjoining to the City
  Shall stay with us. Order for sea is given,
  They have put forth the haven:
  Where their appointment we may best discover,
  And look on their endeavour.

                         Exeunt.

IV. 11

Enter Cæsar, and his Army.

CÆSAR: But being charg'd, we will be still by land,
  Which as I take 't we shall, for his best force
  Is forth to man his galleys. To the vales,
  And hold our best advantage.

                         Exeunt.

IV. 12

Alarum afar off, as at a sea-fight.
Enter Antony, and Scarus.

ANTONY: Yet they are not join'd:
  Where yond pine does stand, I shall discover all.
  I 'll bring thee word straight, how 'tis like to go.
                         Exit.

SCARUS: Swallows have built
  In Cleopatra's sails their nests. The auguries
  Say, they know not, they cannot tell, look grimly,
  And dare not speak their knowledge. Antony,
  Is valiant, and dejected, and by starts
  His fretted fortunes give him hope and fear
  Of what he has, and has not.
                Enter Antony.

ANTONY: All is lost:
  This foul Egyptian hath betrayed me:
  My fleet hath yielded to the foe, and yonder
  They cast their caps up, and carouse together
  Like friends long lost. Triple-turn'd whore, 'tis thou
  Hast sold me to this novice, and my heart
  Makes only wars on thee. Bid them all fly:
  For when I am reveng'd upon my charm,
  I have done all. Bid them all fly, begone.
                Exit Scarus.

  Oh Sun, thy uprise shall I see no more,
  Fortune, and Antony part here, even here
  Do we shake hands? All come to this? The hearts
  That spaniel'd me at heels, to whom I gave
  Their wishes, do discandy, melt their sweets
  On blossoming Cæsar: and this pine is bark'd,
  That overtopp'd them all. Betray'd I am.
  Oh this false soul of Egypt! this grave charm,
  Whose eye beck'd forth my wars, and call'd them home:
  Whose bosom was my crownet, my chief end,
  Like a right Gipsy, hath at fast and loose
  Beguil'd me, to the very heart of loss.
  What Eros, Eros?
                Enter Cleopatra.
  Ah, thou spell! Avaunt.

CLEOPATRA: Why is my Lord enrag'd against his Love?
ANTONY: Vanish, or I shall give thee thy deserving,
  And blemish Cæsar's triumph. Let him take thee,
  And hoist thee up to the shouting plebeians,
  Follow his chariot, like the greatest spot
  Of all thy sex. Most monster-like be shown
  For poor'st diminutives, for dolts, and let
  Patient Octavia, plough thy visage up
  With her prepared nails.

Exit Cleopatra.

  'Tis well thou 'rt gone,
  If it be well to live. But better 'twere
  Thou fell'st into my fury, for one death
  Might have prevented many. Eros, hoa?
  The shirt of Nessus is upon me, teach me
  Alcides, thou mine ancestor, thy rage.
  Let me lodge Lichas on the horns o' th' Moon,
  And with those hands that grasp'd the heaviest club,
  Subdue my worthiest self: the witch shall die.
  To the young Roman boy she hath sold me, and I fall
  Under this plot: she dies for 't. Eros hoa?

Exit.

IV. 13

Enter Cleopatra, Charmian, Iras, and Mardian.
CLEOPATRA: Help me my women: oh he 's more mad
  Than Telamon for his shield, the boar of Thessaly
  Was never so emboss'd.
CHARMIAN: To th' Monument, there lock yourself,
  And send him word you are dead:
  The soul and body rive not more in parting,
  Than greatness going off.

CLEOPATRA: To th' Monument:
  Mardian, go tell him I have slain myself:
  Say, that the last I spoke was Antony,
  And word it (prithee) piteously. Hence Mardian,
  And bring me how he take my death: to th' Monument.
                    Exeunt.

IV. 14

Enter Antony and Eros.

ANTONY: Eros, thou yet behold'st me?
EROS: Ay noble Lord.
ANTONY: Sometime we see a cloud that 's dragonish,
  A vapour sometime, like a bear, or lion,
  A tower'd citadel, a pendent rock,
  A forked mountain, or blue promontory
  With trees upon 't, that nod unto the world,
  And mock our eyes with air.
  Thou hast seen these signs,
  They are black Vesper's pageants.
EROS: Ay my Lord.
ANTONY: That which is now a horse, even with a thought
  The rack dislimns, and makes it indistinct
  As water is in water.
EROS: It does my Lord.
ANTONY: My good knave Eros, now thy Captain is
  Even such a body: here I am Antony,
  Yet cannot hold this visible shape, my knave.
  I made these wars for Egypt, and the Queen,
  Whose heart I thought I had, for she had mine:
  Which whilst it was mine, had annex'd unto 't
  A million moe, (now lost): she Eros has
  Pack'd cards with Cæsar, and false play'd my glory

Unto an enemy's triumph.
Nay, weep not gentle Eros, there is left us
Ourselves to end ourselves.

Enter Mardian.

Oh thy vile Lady, she has robb'd me of my sword.

MARDIAN: No Antony,
My Mistress lov'd thee, and her fortunes mingled
With thine entirely.

ANTONY: Hence saucy Eunuch peace, she hath betray'd me,
And shall die the death.

MARDIAN: Death of one person, can be paid but once,
And that she has discharg'd. What thou wouldst do
Is done unto thy hand: the last she spake
Was Antony, most noble Antony.
Then in the midst a tearing groan did break
The name of Antony: it was divided
Between her heart, and lips: she render'd life
Thy name so buried in her.

ANTONY: Dead then?

MARDIAN: Dead.

ANTONY: Unarm Eros, the long day's task is done,
And we must sleep: that thou depart'st hence safe
Does pay thy labour richly: go.

Exit Mardian.

Off, pluck off,
The seven-fold shield of Ajax cannot keep
The battery from my heart. Oh cleave my sides.
Heart, once be stronger than thy continent,
Crack thy frail case. Apace Eros, apace;
No more a soldier: bruised pieces go,
You have been nobly borne. From me awhile.

Exit Eros.

I will o'ertake thee Cleopatra, and

Weep for my pardon. So it must be, for now
All length is torture: since the torch is out,
Lie down and stray no farther. Now all labour
Mars what it does: yea, very force entangles
Itself with strength: seal then and all is done.
Eros? I come my Queen. Eros? Stay for me,
Where souls do couch on flowers, we 'll hand in hand,
And with our sprightly port make the ghosts gaze:
Dido, and her Æneas shall want troops,
And all the haunt be ours. Come Eros, Eros.

Enter Eros.

EROS: What would my Lord?

ANTONY: Since Cleopatra died,
I have liv'd in such dishonour, that the Gods
Detest my baseness. I, that with my sword,
Quarter'd the World, and o'er green Neptune's back
With ships, made cities, condemn myself, to lack
The courage of a woman, less noble mind
Than she which by her death, our Cæsar tells
I am conqueror of myself. Thou art sworn Eros,
That when the exigent should come, which now
Is come indeed: when I should see behind me
Th' inevitable prosecution of disgrace and horror,
That on my command, thou then wouldst kill me.
Do 't, the time is come: thou strik'st not me,
'Tis Cæsar thou defeat'st. Put colour in thy cheek.

EROS: The Gods withhold me,
Shall I do that which all the Parthian darts,
(Though enemy) lost aim, and could not.

ANTONY: Eros,
Wouldst thou be window'd in great Rome, and see
Thy Master thus with pleach'd arms, bending down
His corrigible neck, his face subdu'd

To penetrative shame; whilst the wheel'd seat
Of fortunate Cæsar drawn before him, branded
His baseness that ensued.

EROS: I would not see 't.

ANTONY: Come then: for with a wound I must be cur'd.
Draw that thy honest sword, which thou hast worn
Most useful for thy country.

EROS: Oh sir, pardon me.

ANTONY: When I did make thee free, swor'st thou not
then
To do this when I bad thee? Do it at once,
Or thy precedent services are all
But accidents unpurpos'd. Draw, and come.

EROS: Turn from me then that noble countenance,
Wherein the worship of the whole world lies.

ANTONY: Lo thee.

EROS: My sword is drawn.

ANTONY: Then let it do at once
The thing why thou hast drawn it.

EROS: My dear Master,
My Captain, and my Emperor. Let me say
Before I strike this bloody stroke, farewell.

ANTONY: 'Tis said man, and farewell.

EROS: Farewell great Chief. Shall I strike now?

ANTONY: Now Eros.

EROS: Why there then:

Kills himself.

Thus I do escape the sorrow of Antony's death.

ANTONY: Thrice-nobler than myself,
Thou teachest me: oh valiant Eros, what
I should, and thou couldst not, my Queen and Eros
Have by their brave instruction got upon me
A nobleness in record. But I will be

A bridegroom in my death, and run into 't
As to a lover's bed. Come then, and Eros,
Thy Master dies thy scholar; to do thus
I learn'd of thee. How, not dead? not dead?
The guard, how? Oh dispatch me.

Enter Dercetas and a Guard.

1 GUARD: What 's the noise?

ANTONY: I have done my work ill friends:
Oh make an end of what I have begun.

2 GUARD: The star is fall'n.

1 GUARD: And time is at his period.

ALL: Alas, and woe.

ANTONY: Let him that loves me, strike me dead.

1 GUARD: Not I.

2 GUARD: Nor I.

3 GUARD: Nor any one.

Exeunt Guard.

DERCETAS: Thy death and fortunes bid thy followers fly.
This sword but shown to Cæsar, with this tidings,
Shall enter me with him.

Enter Diomedes.

DIOMEDES: Where 's Antony?

DERCETAS: There Diomed there.

DIOMEDES: Lives he? wilt thou not answer man?

Exit Dercetas.

ANTONY: Art thou there Diomed?
Draw thy sword, and give me,
Sufficing strokes for death.

DIOMEDES: Most absolute Lord:
My Mistress Cleopatra sent me to thee.

ANTONY: When did she send thee?

DIOMEDES: Now my Lord.

ANTONY: Where is she?

DIOMEDES : Lock'd in her Monument : she had a prophesy-
   ing fear
Of what hath come to pass : for when she saw
(Which never shall be found) you did suspect
She had dispos'd with Cæsar, and that your rage
Would not be purg'd, she sent you word she was dead :
But fearing since how it might work, hath sent
Me to proclaim the truth, and I am come
I dread, too late.

ANTONY : Too late good Diomed : call my guard I prithee.

DIOMEDES : What hoa : the Emperor's guard,
   The guard, what hoa ? Come, your Lord calls.
     Enter four or five of the Guard of Antony.

ANTONY : Bear me good friends where Cleopatra bides,
   'Tis the last service that I shall command you.

1 GUARD : Woe, woe are we sir, you may not live to wear
   All your true followers out.

ALL : Most heavy day.

ANTONY : Nay good my fellows, do not please sharp fate
   To grace it with your sorrows. Bid that welcome
   Which comes to punish us, and we punish it
   Seeming to bear it lightly. Take me up,
   I have led you oft, carry me now good friends,
   And have my thanks for all.
     Exeunt bearing Antony.

IV. 15

*Enter Cleopatra, and her Maids aloft, with Charmian,
and Iras.*

CLEOPATRA : Oh Charmian, I will never go from hence.

CHARMIAN : Be comforted dear Madam.

CLEOPATRA : No, I will not :

All strange and terrible events are welcome,
But comforts we despise; our size of sorrow
Proportion'd to our cause, must be as great
As that which makes it.

Enter Diomedes.

How now? is he dead?

DIOMEDES: His death 's upon him, but not dead.
Look out o' th' other side your Monument,
His guard have brought him thither.

Enter Antony, and the Guard.

CLEOPATRA: Oh Sun,
Burn the great sphere thou mov'st in, darkling stand
The varying shore o' th' world. O Antony, Antony,
Antony!
Help Charmian, help Iras help: help friends
Below, let's draw him hither.

ANTONY: Peace.
Not Cæsar's valour hath o'erthrown Antony,
But Antony's hath triumph'd on itself.

CLEOPATRA: So it should be,
That none but Antony should conquer Antony,
But woe 'tis so.

ANTONY: I am dying Egypt, dying; only
I here importune death awhile, until
Of many thousand kisses, the poor last
I lay upon thy lips.

CLEOPATRA: I dare not dear,
Dear my Lord pardon: I dare not,
Lest I be taken: not th' imperious show
Of the full-fortun'd Cæsar, ever shall
Be brooch'd with me, if knife, drugs, serpents have
Edge, sting, or operation. I am safe:
Your wife Octavia, with her modest eyes,

And still conclusion, shall acquire no honour
Demuring upon me: but come, come Antony,
Help me my women, we must draw thee up:
Assist good friends.

ANTONY: Oh quick, or I am gone.

CLEOPATRA: Here 's sport indeed:
How heavy weighs my Lord?
Our strength is all gone into heaviness,
That makes the weight. Had I great Juno's power,
The strong wing'd Mercury should fetch thee up,
And set thee by Jove's side. Yet come a little,
Wishers were ever fools. Oh come, come, come,

They heave Antony aloft to Cleopatra.

And welcome, welcome. Die where thou hast liv'd,
Quicken with kissing: had my lips that power,
Thus would I wear them out.

ALL: A heavy sight.

ANTONY: I am dying Egypt, dying.
Give me some wine, and let me speak a little.

CLEOPATRA: No, let me speak, and let me rail so high,
That the false housewife Fortune, break her wheel,
Provok'd by my offence.

ANTONY: One word, sweet Queen:
Of Cæsar seek your honour, with your safety. Oh.

CLEOPATRA: They do not go together.

ANTONY: Gentle hear me,
None about Cæsar trust, but Proculeius.

CLEOPATRA: My resolution, and my hands, I'll trust,
None about Cæsar.

ANTONY: The miserable change now at my end,
Lament nor sorrow at: but please your thoughts
In feeding them with those my former fortunes
Wherein I lived. The greatest Prince o' th' world,

The noblest: and do now not basely die,
Not cowardly put off my helmet to
My countryman. A Roman, by a Roman
Valiantly vanquish'd. Now my spirit is going,
I can do no more.

CLEOPATRA: Noblest of men, woo't die?
Hast thou no care of me, shall I abide
In this dull world, which in thy absence is
No better than a sty? Oh see my women:

Antony dies.

The Crown o' th' earth doth melt. My Lord?
Oh wither'd is the garland of the war,
The soldier's pole is fall'n: young boys and girls
Are level now with men: the odds is gone,
And there is nothing left remarkable
Beneath the visiting Moon.

CHARMIAN: Oh quietness, Lady.

IRAS: She 's dead too, our Sovereign.

CHARMIAN: Lady.

IRAS: Madam.

CHARMIAN: Oh Madam, Madam, Madam.

IRAS: Royal Egypt: Empress.

CHARMIAN: Peace, peace, Iras.

CLEOPATRA: No more but e'en a woman, and commanded
By such poor passion, as the maid that milks,
And does the meanest chares. It were for me,
To throw my sceptre at the injurious Gods,
To tell them that this World did equal theirs,
Till they had stol'n our jewel. All 's but naught:
Patience is sottish, and impatience does
Become a dog that 's mad: then is it sin,
To rush into the secret house of death,

Ere death dare come to us? How do you women?
What, what good cheer? Why how now Charmian?
My noble girls? Ah women, women! Look
Our lamp is spent, it 's out. Good sirs, take heart,
We 'll bury him: and then, what 's brave, what 's noble,
Let 's do it after the high Roman fashion,
And make death proud to take us. Come, away,
This case of that huge spirit now is cold,
Ah women, women! Come, we have no friend
But resolution, and the briefest end.

Exeunt, bearing off Antony's body.

V . I

Enter Cæsar, Agrippa, Dolabella, Mæcenas, with his
Council of War.

CÆSAR: Go to him Dolabella, bid him yield,
Being so frustrate, tell him,
He mocks the pauses that he makes.

DOLABELLA: Cæsar, I shall.

Exit.

Enter Dercetas with the sword of Antony.

CÆSAR: Wherefore is that? And what art thou that dar'st
Appear thus to us?

DERCETAS: I am call'd Dercetas,
Mark Antony I serv'd, who best was worthy
Best to be serv'd: whilst he stood up, and spoke
He was my Master, and I wore my life
To spend upon his haters. If thou please
To take me to thee, as I was to him,
I'll be to Cæsar: if thou pleasest not, I yield thee up my
life.

CÆSAR: What is 't thou say'st?

DERCETAS: I say, Oh Cæsar, Antony is dead.

CÆSAR: The breaking of so great a thing should make
  A greater crack. The round World
  Should have shook lions into civil streets,
  And citizens to their dens. The death of Antony
  Is not a single doom, in the name lay
  A moiety of the world.

DERCETAS: He is dead Cæsar,
  Not by a public minister of justice,
  Nor by a hired knife, but that self hand
  Which writ his honour in the acts it did,
  Hath with the courage which the heart did lend it,
  Splitted the heart. This is his sword,
  I robb'd his wound of it: behold it stain'd
  With his most noble blood.

CÆSAR: Look you sad friends,
  The Gods rebuke me, but it is tidings
  To wash the eyes of Kings.

AGRIPPA: And strange it is,
  That Nature must compel us to lament
  Our most persisted deed.

MÆCENAS: His taints and honours, wag'd equal with him.

AGRIPPA: A rarer spirit never
  Did steer humanity: but you Gods will give us
  Some faults to make us men. Cæsar is touch'd.

MÆCENAS: When such a spacious mirror's set before him.
  He needs must see himself.

CÆSAR: Oh Antony,
  I have followed thee to this, but we do lance
  Diseases in our bodies. I must perforce
  Have shown to thee such a declining day,
  Or look on thine: we could not stall together,
  In the whole world. But yet let me lament

With tears as sovereign as the blood of hearts,
That thou my brother, my competitor,
In top of all design; my mate in empire,
Friend and companion in the front of war,
The arm of mine own body, and the heart
Where mine his thoughts did kindle; that our stars
Unreconcilable, should divide our equalness to this.
Hear me good friends,
But I will tell you at some meeter season,
The business of this man looks out of him,
We'll hear him what he says.

Enter an Egyptian.

Whence are you?

EGYPTIAN: A poor Egyptian yet, the Queen my Mistress
Confin'd in all she has, her Monument,
Of thy intents, desires instruction,
That she preparedly may frame herself
To th' way she 's forc'd to.

CÆSAR: Bid her have good heart,
She soon shall know of us, by some of ours,
How honourable, and how kindly we
Determine for her. For Cæsar cannot leave to be ungentle.

EGYPTIAN: So the Gods preserve thee.

Exit.

CÆSAR: Come hither Proculeius. Go and say
We purpose her no shame: give her what comforts
The quality of her passion shall require;
Lest in her greatness, by some mortal stroke
She do defeat us. For her life in Rome,
Would be eternal in our triumph: go,
And with your speediest bring us what she says,
And how you find of her.

PROCULEIUS: Cæsar I shall.

Exit Proculeius.

CÆSAR: Gallus, go you along: where 's Dolabella, to
   second Proculeius?

ALL: Dolabella.

CÆSAR: Let him alone: for I remember now
   How he 's employ'd: he shall in time be ready.
   Go with me to my tent, where you shall see
   How hardly I was drawn into this war,
   How calm and gentle I proceeded still
   In all my writings. Go with me, and see
   What I can show in this.

Exeunt.

V. 2

Enter Cleopatra, Charmian, Iras, and Mardian.

CLEOPATRA: My desolation does begin to make
   A better life: 'tis paltry to be Cæsar:
   Not being Fortune, he 's but Fortune's knave.
   A minister of her will: and it is great
   To do that thing that ends all other deeds,
   Which shackles accidents, and bolts up change;
   Which sleeps, and never palates more the dung,
   The beggar's nurse, and Cæsar's.

Enter Proculeius.

PROCULEIUS: Cæsar sends greeting to the Queen of
   Egypt,
   And bids thee study on what fair demands
   Thou mean'st to have him grant thee.

CLEOPATRA: What 's thy name?

PROCULEIUS: My name is Proculeius.

CLEOPATRA: Antony
  Did tell me of you, bade me trust you, but
  I do not greatly care to be deceiv'd
  That have no use for trusting. If your Master
  Would have a Queen his beggar, you must tell him,
  That Majesty to keep decorum, must
  No less beg than a Kingdom: if he please
  To give me conquer'd Egypt for my son,
  He gives me so much of mine own, as I
  Will kneel to him with thanks.
PROCULEIUS: Be of good cheer:
  You 're fall'n into a princely hand, fear nothing,
  Make your full reference freely to my Lord,
  Who is so full of grace, that it flows over
  On all that need. Let me report to him
  Your sweet dependency, and you shall find
  A conqueror that will pray in aid for kindness,
  Where he for grace is kneel'd to.
CLEOPATRA: Pray you tell him,
  I am his Fortune's vassal, and I send him
  The greatness he has got. I hourly learn
  A doctrine of obedience, and would gladly
  Look him i' th' face.
PROCULEIUS: This I 'll report dear Lady.
  Have comfort, for I know your plight is pitied
  Of him that caus'd it.
                    Enter soldiers.
  You see how easily she may be surpris'd:
  Guard her till Cæsar come.
IRAS: Royal Queen.
CHARMIAN: Oh Cleopatra, thou art taken Queen.
CLEOPATRA: Quick, quick, good hands.
PROCULEIUS: Hold worthy Lady, hold:

Do not yourself such wrong, who are in this
Reliev'd, but not betray'd.

CLEOPATRA: What of death too that rids our dogs of
languish?

PROCULEIUS: Cleopatra, do not abuse my Masters'
bounty, by
Th' undoing of yourself: let the World see
His nobleness well acted, which your death
Will never let come forth.

CLEOPATRA: Where art thou Death?
Come hither come; come, come, and take a Queen
Worth many babes and beggars.

PROCULEIUS: Oh temperance Lady.

CLEOPATRA: Sir, I will eat no meat, I 'll not drink sir,
If idle talk will once be necessary
I 'll not sleep neither. This mortal house I 'll ruin,
Do Cæsar what he can. Know sir, that I
Will not wait pinion'd at your Master's Court,
Nor once be chastis'd with the sober eye
Of dull Octavia. Shall they hoist me up,
And show me to the shouting varletry
Of censuring Rome? Rather a ditch in Egypt
Be gentle grave unto me, rather on Nilus' mud
Lay me stark-naked, and let the water-flies
Blow me into abhorring; rather make
My country's high pyramides my gibbet,
And hang me up in chains.

PROCULEIUS: You do extend
These thoughts of horror further than you shall
Find cause in Cæsar.

Enter Dolabella.

DOLABELLA: Proculeius,
What thou hast done, thy Master Cæsar knows,

And he hath sent for thee: for the Queen,
I 'll take her to my guard.

PROCULEIUS: So Dolabella,
It shall content me best: be gentle to her,
To Cæsar I will speak, what you shall please.
If you'll employ me to him.

CLEOPATRA: Say, I would die.

Exit Proculeius.

DOLABELLA: Most noble Empress, you have heard of me.

CLEOPATRA: I cannot tell.

DOLABELLA: Assuredly you know me.

CLEOPATRA: No matter, sir, what I have heard or known:
You laugh when boys or women tell their dreams,
Is 't not your trick?

DOLABELLA: I understand not, Madam.

CLEOPATRA: I dreamt there was an Emperor Antony.
Oh such another sleep, that I might see
But such another man.

DOLABELLA: If it might please ye.

CLEOPATRA: His face was as the Heav'ns, and therein
stuck
A Sun and Moon, which kept their course, and lighted
The little o' th' earth.

DOLABELLA: Most sovereign creature.

CLEOPATRA: His legs bestrid the Ocean: his rear'd arm
Crested the world: his voice was propertied
As all the tuned spheres, and that to friends:
But when he meant to quail, and shake the Orb,
He was as rattling thunder. For his bounty,
There was no winter in 't. An Antony it was,
That grew the more by reaping: his delights
Were dolphin-like, they show'd his back above
The element they liv'd in: in his livery

Walk'd crowns and crownets: realms and islands were
As plates dropp'd from his pocket.

DOLABELLA: Cleopatra.

CLEOPATRA: Think you there was, or might be such a man
As this I dreamt of?

DOLABELLA: Gentle Madam, no.

CLEOPATRA: You lie up to the hearing of the Gods:
But if there be, nor ever were one such
It's past the size of dreaming: Nature wants stuff
To vie strange forms with fancy, yet t' imagine
An Antony were Nature's piece, 'gainst Fancy,
Condemning shadows quite.

DOLABELLA: Hear me, good Madam:
Your loss is as yourself, great; and you bear it
As answering to the weight: would I might never
O'ertake pursu'd success, but I do feel
By the rebound of yours, a grief that smites
My very heart at root.

CLEOPATRA: I thank you sir:
Know you what Cæsar means to do with me?

DOLABELLA: I am loath to tell you what, I would you
knew.

CLEOPATRA: Nay pray you sir.

DOLABELLA: Though he be honourable.

CLEOPATRA: He 'll lead me then in triumph.

DOLABELLA: Madam he will, I know 't.

Flourish.
Enter Proculeius, Cæsar, Gallus, Mæcenas,
and others of his Train.

ALL: Make way there, Cæsar.

CÆSAR: Which is the Queen of Egypt.

DOLABELLA: It is the Emperor Madam.
Cleopatra kneels.

CÆSAR: Arise, you shall not kneel:
I pray you rise, rise Egypt.

CLEOPATRA: Sir, the Gods will have it thus,
My Master and my Lord I must obey.

CÆSAR: Take to you no hard thoughts,
The record of what injuries you did us,
Though written in our flesh, we shall remember
As things but done by chance.

CLEOPATRA: Sole Sir o' th' World,
I cannot project mine own cause so well
To make it clear, but do confess I have
Been laden with like frailties, which before
Have often sham'd our sex.

CÆSAR: Cleopatra know,
We will extenuate rather than enforce:
If you apply yourself to our intents,
Which towards you are most gentle, you shall find
A benefit in this change: but if you seek
To lay on me a cruelty, by taking
Antony's course, you shall bereave yourself
Of my good purposes, and put your children
To that destruction which I 'll guard them from,
If thereon you rely. I 'll take my leave.

CLEOPATRA: And may through all the world: 'tis yours,
and we
Your scutcheons, and your signs of conquest shall
Hang in what place you please. Here my good Lord.

CÆSAR: You shall advise me in all for Cleopatra.

CLEOPATRA: This is the brief: of money, plate, and jewels
I am possess'd of, 'tis exactly valued,
Not petty things admitted. Where's Seleucus?

SELEUCUS: Here Madam.

CLEOPATRA: This is my Treasurer, let him speak, my Lord,

Upon this peril, that I have reserv'd
To myself nothing. Speak the truth Seleucus.

SELEUCUS: Madam, I had rather seel my lips,
Than to my peril speak that which is not.

CLEOPATRA: What have I kept back?

SELEUCUS: Enough to purchase what you have made
known.

CÆSAR: Nay blush not Cleopatra, I approve
Your wisdom in the deed.

CLEOPATRA: See Cæsar: Oh behold,
How pomp is followed: mine will now be yours,
And should we shift estates, yours would be mine.
The ingratitude of this Seleucus, does
Even make me wild. Oh slave, of no more trust
Than love that's hir'd? What goest thou back, thou shalt
Go back I warrant thee: but I'll catch thine eyes
Though they had wings. Slave, soulless, villain, dog.
O rarely base!

CÆSAR: Good Queen, let us entreat you.

CLEOPATRA: O Cæsar, what a wounding shame is this,
That thou vouchsafing here to visit me,
Doing the honour of thy lordliness
To one so meek, that mine own servant should
Parcel the sum of my disgraces, by
Addition of his envy. Say, good Cæsar,
That I some lady trifles have reserv'd,
Immoment toys, things of such dignity
As we greet modern friends withal, and say
Some nobler token I have kept apart
For Livia and Octavia, to induce
Their mediation, must I be unfolded
With one that I have bred: the Gods! it smites me
Beneath the fall I have. Prithee go hence,

Or I shall show the cinders of my spirits
Through th' ashes of my chance: wert thou a man,
Thou wouldst have mercy on me.

CÆSAR: Forbear Seleucus.

CLEOPATRA: Be it known, that we the greatest are mis-
thought
For things that others do: and when we fall,
We answer others' merits, in our name,
Are therefore to be pitied.

CÆSAR: Cleopatra,
Not what you have reserv'd, nor what acknowledg'd
Put we i' th' roll of conquest: still be 't yours,
Bestow it at your pleasure, and believe
Cæsar's no merchant, to make prize with you
Of things that merchants sold. Therefore be cheer'd,
Make not your thoughts your prisons: no dear Queen,
For we intend so to dispose you, as
Yourself shall give us counsel: feed, and sleep:
Our care and pity is so much upon you,
That we remain your friend, and so adieu.

CLEOPATRA: My Master, and my Lord.

CÆSAR: Not so: adieu.

Flourish.
Exeunt Cæsar and his train.

CLEOPATRA: He words me girls, he words me,
That I should not be noble to myself.
But hark thee Charmian.

IRAS: Finish good Lady, the bright day is done,
And we are for the dark.

CLEOPATRA: Hie thee again,
I have spoke already, and it is provided,
Go put it to the haste.

CHARMIAN: Madam I will.

Enter Dolabella.

DOLABELLA: Where is the Queen?

CHARMIAN: Behold sir.

Exit.

CLEOPATRA: Dolabella.

DOLABELLA: Madam, as thereto sworn, by your command

(Which my love makes religion to obey)

I tell you this: Cæsar through Syria

Intends his journey, and within three days,

You with your children will he send before,

Make your best use of this. I have perform'd

Your pleasure, and my promise.

CLEOPATRA: Dolabella, I shall remain your debtor.

DOLABELLA: I your servant:

Adieu good Queen, I must attend on Cæsar.

Exit.

CLEOPATRA: Farewell, and thanks.

Now Iras, what think'st thou?

Thou, an Egyptian puppet shall be shown

In Rome as well as I: mechanic slaves

With greasy aprons, rules, and hammers shall

Uplift us to the view. In their thick breaths,

Rank of gross diet, shall we be enclouded,

And forc'd to drink their vapour.

IRAS: The Gods forbid.

CLEOPATRA: Nay, 'tis most certain Iras: saucy lictors

Will catch at us like strumpets, and scald rhymers

Ballad us out a' tune. The quick comedians

Extemporally will stage us, and present

Our Alexandrian revels: Antony

Shall be brought drunken forth, and I shall see

Some squeaking Cleopatra boy my greatness

I' th' posture of a whore.

IRAS: O the good Gods!

CLEOPATRA: Nay that 's certain.

IRAS: I 'll never see 't! for I am sure mine nails
Are stronger than mine eyes.

CLEOPATRA: Why that 's the way to fool their prepara-
tion,
And to conquer their most absurd intents.
Enter Charmian.
Now Charmian.
Show me my women like a Queen: go fetch
My best attires. I am again for Cydnus,
To meet Mark Antony. Sirrah Iras, go
(Now noble Charmian, we 'll dispatch indeed)
And when thou hast done this chare, I 'll give thee leave
To play till Doomsday: bring our Crown, and all.
Exit Iras. A noise within.
Wherefore 's this noise?
Enter a Guardsman.

GUARDSMAN: Here is a rural fellow,
That will not be denied your Highness' presence,
He brings you figs.

CLEOPATRA: Let him come in.
Exit Guardsman.
What poor an instrument
May do a noble deed: he brings me liberty:
My resolution 's plac'd, and I have nothing
Of woman in me: now from head to foot
I am marble-constant: now the fleeting Moon
No planet is of mine.
Enter Guardsman, and Clown.

GUARDSMAN: This is the man.

CLEOPATRA: Avoid, and leave him.

Exit Guardsman.

Hast thou the pretty worm of Nilus there,
That kills and pains not?

CLOWN: Truly I have him: but I would not be the party
that should desire you to touch him, for his biting is
immortal: those that do die of it, do seldom or never
recover.

CLEOPATRA: Remember'st thou any that have died on 't?

CLOWN: Very many, men and women too. I heard of one
of them no longer than yesterday, a very honest woman,
but something given to lie, as a woman should not do,
but in the way of honesty, how she died of the biting of it,
what pain she felt: truly, she makes a very good report
o' th' worm: but he that will believe all that they say,
shall never be saved by half that they do: but this is most
falliable, the worm's an odd worm.

CLEOPATRA: Get thee hence, farewell.

CLOWN: I wish you all joy of the worm.

CLEOPATRA: Farewell.

CLOWN: You must think this (look you), that the worm
will do his kind.

CLEOPATRA: Ay, ay, farewell.

CLOWN: Look you, the worm is not to be trusted, but in
the keeping of wise people: for indeed, there is no
goodness in the worm.

CLEOPATRA: Take thou no care, it shall be heeded.

CLOWN: Very good: give it nothing I pray you, for it is
not worth the feeding.

CLEOPATRA: Will it eat me?

CLOWN: You must not think I am so simple, but I know
the devil himself will not eat a woman: I know, that a
woman is a dish for the Gods, if the devil dress her not.
But truly, these same whoreson devils do the Gods great

harm in their women: for in every ten that they make,
the devils mar five.

CLEOPATRA: Well, get thee gone, farewell.

CLOWN: Yes forsooth: I wish you joy o' th' worm.

Exit.

Enter Iras.

CLEOPATRA: Give me my Robe, put on my Crown, I
    have
Immortal longings in me. Now no more
The juice of Egypt's grape shall moist this lip.
Yare, yare, good Iras; quick: methinks I hear
Antony call, I see him rouse himself
To praise my noble act. I hear him mock
The luck of Cæsar, which the Gods give men
To excuse their after wrath. Husband, I come:
Now to that name, my courage prove my title.
I am fire, and air; my other elements
I give to baser life. So, have you done?
Come then, and take the last warmth of my lips.
Farewell kind Charmian, Iras, long farewell.

Iras falls.

Have I the aspic in my lips? Dost fall?
If thou, and Nature can so gently part,
The stroke of death is as a lover's pinch,
Which hurts, and is desir'd. Dost thou lie still?
If thus thou vanishest, thou tell'st the world,
It is not worth leave-taking.

CHARMIAN: Dissolve thick cloud, and rain, that I may say
The Gods themselves do weep.

CLEOPATRA: This proves me base:
If she first meet the curled Antony,
He 'll make demand of her, and spend that kiss
Which is my heaven to have. Come thou mortal wretch,

With thy sharp teeth this knot intrinsicate,
Of life at once untie: poor venomous fool,
Be angry and dispatch. Oh couldst thou speak,
That I might hear thee call great Cæsar ass, unpolicied.

CHARMIAN: Oh Eastern Star.

CLEOPATRA: Peace, peace:
Dost thou not see my baby at my breast,
That sucks the nurse asleep.

CHARMIAN: O break! O break!

CLEOPATRA: As sweet as balm, as soft as air, as gentle.
O Antony! Nay I will take thee too.
What should I stay—

Dies.

CHARMIAN: In this wild world? So fare thee well:
Now boast thee Death, in thy possession lies
A lass unparallel'd. Downy windows close,
And golden Phœbus, never be beheld
Of eyes again so royal: your Crown's awry,
I'll mend it, and then play—

Enter the Guard, rustling in.

1 GUARD: Where's the Queen?

CHARMIAN: Speak softly, wake her not.

1 GUARD: Cæsar hath sent—

CHARMIAN: Too slow a messenger.
Oh come apace, dispatch, I partly feel thee.

1 GUARD: Approach hoa,
All's not well: Cæsar's beguil'd.

2 GUARD: There's Dolabella sent from Cæsar: call him.

1 GUARD: What work is here Charmian?
Is this well done?

CHARMIAN: It is well done, and fitting for a Princess
Descended of so many royal Kings.
Ah soldier.

Charmian dies.
Enter Dolabella.

DOLABELLA: How goes it here?

2 GUARD: All dead.

DOLABELLA: Cæsar, thy thoughts
Touch their effects in this: thyself art coming
To see perform'd the dreaded act which thou
So sought'st to hinder.

Enter Cæsar and all his train, marching.

ALL: A way there, a way for Cæsar.

DOLABELLA: Oh sir, you are too sure an augurer:
That you did fear, is done.

CÆSAR: Bravest at the last,
She levell'd at our purposes, and being royal
Took her own way: the manner of their deaths,
I do not see them bleed.

DOLABELLA: Who was last with them?

1 GUARD: A simple countryman, that brought her figs:
This was his basket.

CÆSAR: Poison'd then.

1 GUARD: Oh Cæsar:
This Charmian liv'd but now, she stood and spake:
I found her trimming up the diadem
On her dead mistress; tremblingly she stood,
And on the sudden dropp'd.

CÆSAR: Oh noble weakness:
If they had swallow'd poison, 'twould appear
By external swelling: but she looks like sleep,
As she would catch another Antony
In her strong toil of grace.

DOLABELLA: Here on her breast,
There is a vent of blood, and something blown,
The like is on her arm.

1 GUARD: This is an aspic's trail,
    And these fig-leaves have slime upon them, such
    As th' aspic leaves upon the caves of Nile.
CÆSAR: Most probable
    That so she died: for her physician tells me
    She hath pursu'd conclusions infinite
    Of easy ways to die. Take up her bed,
    And bear her women from the Monument,
    She shall be buried by her Antony.
    No grave upon the earth shall clip in it
    A pair so famous: high events as these
    Strike those that make them: and their story is
    No less in pity, than his glory which
    Brought them to be lamented. Our army shall
    In solemn show, attend this funeral,
    And then to Rome. Come Dolabella, see
    High order, in this great solemnity.
                Exeunt Omnes.

NOTES

References are to the page and line of this edition;
there are 33 lines to the full page.

office and devotion of their view: gazing with devoted P. 23 L 8
service.

reneges all temper: denies all restraint. P. 23 L. II

bellows and the fan: i.e. alternately rousing and allay- P. 23 L .12
ing.

gipsy: Egyptian. Gipsies were thought to have come P. 23 L. 14
from Egypt. Shakespeare regards Cleopatra as a
dusky queen: actually she was of Macedonian blood.

Look where they come: A phrase common in Eliza- P. 23 L. 17
bethan plays to draw attention to characters entering
at the back of the stage.

triple pillar: Antony, with Octavius and Lepidus, was P. 23 L. 19
one of the three triumvirs who between them ruled
the Roman world after Julius Cæsar's death.

Fulvia: Antony's legal wife. P. 23 L. 30

process: a legal summons to appear before a court of P. 24 L. 8
law.

the wide arch Of the rang'd Empire fall: This is one of P. 24 L. 14
the many concentrated phrases in this play which
convey their meaning emotionally and are so difficult to paraphrase. The image is of the sweep of a
great arch, stone supporting stone.

here is my space: i.e. in the compass of Cleopatra's P. 24 L. 15
arms.

qualities: natures. So Viola says that a professional P. 25 L. 4
fool must 'observe the quality of persons.'

property: that which is proper to. P. 25 L. 9

change his horns with garlands: i.e. be led like a beast P. 25 L. 21
decked out for the sacrifice – with the inevitable joke
on cuckolds, for husbands deceived by their wives

were said to wear horns. *Change*=alter, adorn. Some editors read 'charge'.

P. 25 L. 29   *banquet:* not a formal feast, but wine and light refreshments.

P. 26 L. 14   *Herod of Jewry:* always represented as a ferocious tyrant. Charmian's infant would therefore have character.

P. 26 L. 26   *I forgive thee for a witch:* 'you're no soothsayer.'

P. 27 L. 16   *that cannot go:* see note on *she creeps*, p. 75, l. 29.

P. 28 L. 6   *a Roman thought:* a Roman's sense of duty to Rome.

P. 28 L. 26   *bad news infects the teller:* a messenger of bad news is made to suffer.

P. 29 L. 1   *Extended:* made an extent upon, seized.

P. 29 L. 6   *Speak ... home:* i.e. directly.

P. 29 L. 11   *Oh then we bring forth ... earing:* The general meaning is – 'worthless deeds follow when we do not listen to criticism, but to listen to an account of our misdoings is profitable.' Some editors alter 'winds' to 'minds'. *Earing*=ploughing.

P. 30 L. 3   *By revolution low'ring:* changed to the opposite by the turn of the wheel.

P. 30 L. 15   *death's the word:* they swear that they will die if we go.

P. 30 L. 33   *left unseen ... discredited your travel:* i.e. Cleopatra is one of the sights of Egypt – as the courtesans were of Venice.

P. 31 L. 9   *when it pleaseth ... make new:* 'the gods are like tailors; when one suit is worn out, they can fit a man with a new one.'

P. 31 L. 16   *tears live in an onion:* 'any tears you shed will have to be forced.'

P. 31 L. 24   *what we purpose:* The use of 'we' here shows that Antony assumes the tone of the commander asserting himself.

P. 31 L. 29   *contriving friends:* friends plotting for us.

stands up For the main soldier: i.e. is ambitious to become the supreme soldier. P. 32 L. 4

courser's hair, hath yet but life: It was believed that horse hairs laid in water became alive. P. 32 L. 7

Thou teachest like a fool: Here Cleopatra the expert gives Charmian a lesson in the way to catch a man and keep him. P. 32 L. 29

treasons planted: set in position, like an explosive mine. P. 33 L. 20

none our parts so poor: a reminder of Antony's own words (p. 24, l. 21) 'we stand up peerless'. P. 34 L. 2

Can Fulvia die?: The mistress's bitter sneer that the legal wife lives for ever. P. 34 L. 27

By the fire: i.e. the sun which makes fertile the mud of the Nile. P. 35 L. 5

Cut my lace: Ladies of fashion in Shakespeare's time controlled their figures by lacing themselves within 'busks', or corsets, of whale bone, wood, or even iron. At moments of high emotion drastic relief was sometimes necessary. P. 35 L. 9

this is meetly: 'quite a good effort.' P. 35 L. 22

Herculean Roman ... carriage of his chafe: 'how fine he looks when he is angry.' Antony claimed to be descended from Hercules. P. 35 L. 26

Oh, my oblivion is a very Antony: a cry of pathos, another of Shakespeare's untranslatable phrases – 'even when I forget everything I remember nothing but Antony, though he forgets me.' P. 35 L. 33

my becomings: my natural feelings. P. 36 L. 8

Eye well: seem good. P. 36 L. 9

That thou ... with thee: 'present or absent, you are always with me.' P. 36 L. 16

I must not think ... blackness: 'as the black night shows up the stars, so Antony's good qualities make the bad more conspicuous.' P. 37 L. 1

drums him: calls him to his duty. In Shakespeare's P. 37 L. 20

time the drum, not the bugle, was used to summon soldiers to parade.

P. 37 L. 23   *Pawn their experience … judgement:* indulge in pleasures which by experience and judgement they know to be harmful.

P. 38 L. 3   *primal state:* the very beginning.

P. 38 L. 5   *ebb'd man … lack'd:* the man whose power has slipped away is never loved till he is not worth loving, and becomes precious because of his absence.

P. 38 L. 8   *a vagabond flag … motion:* Editors usually take *flag* to mean the water iris. If so this is the only time Shakespeare uses the word. More probably Shakespeare had in mind some actual flag that he had noticed trailing in the water, carried up and down by the tide until it rotted away. *Lacking* is often emended to 'lackeying' = following like a lackey; but Shakespeare never uses 'lackey' as a verb. 'Lacking' may mean 'now wet, now dry'.

P. 38 L. 27   *gilded puddle:* covered with a yellow film, as in an ill-drained farmyard.

P. 39 L. 20   *for my bond:* for what I am bound to do.

P. 39 L. 26   *mandragora:* a potion prepared from mandrake, used to promote sleep.

P. 40 L. 20   *demi-Atlas:* i.e. one who bears up half the world.

P. 40 L. 26   *Broad-fronted:* with a large forehead.

P. 40 L. 30   *anchor his aspect:* fix his gaze.

P. 41 L. 2   *great medicine … tinct gilded thee:* i.e. *aurum potabile*, tincture of gold, or the grand elixir which alchemists were for ever trying to discover, for it would give perpetual youth.

P. 41 L. 15   *arm-gaunt:* a phrase not satisfactorily explained. If the reading is correct, perhaps it means 'having gaunt limbs.'

P. 41 L. 29   *posts:* messengers. In Shakespeare's time the state maintained a service of post horses which were kept constantly ready at various stages on the main roads.

die a beggar: have bad luck.   **P. 41 L. 33**

paragon: make equal comparison with.   **P. 42 L. 8**

My salad days: when I was green and inexperienced. **P. 42 L. 12**

prorogue his honour: suspend his sense of honour. **P. 43 L. 20**

Good Enobarbus ... : Lepidus is a man of tact, not **P. 44 L. 22**
strength, always trying to avoid unpleasant issues,
and so is the first to drop out of the triumvirate.

Were I the wearer ... shave 't to-day: To pluck his **P. 44 L. 29**
beard was to give a man the greatest possible insult.
So Enobarbus means 'I would dare Cæsar to insult
me.'

private stomaching: personal squabbling.   **P. 44 L. 31**

curstness grow to th' matter: peevishness bring disaster. **P. 45 L. 21**

theme for you: a subject which concerned you. **P. 46 L. 15**

Having alike your cause: 'having the same cause as **P. 46 L. 23**
you.' i.e. 'those who fight against you fight against
me.'

patch a quarrel: quarrel about patches – little incidents. **P. 46 L. 24**

snaffle: i.e. a bit without a curb, used only with a **P. 47 L. 3**
horse easily managed.

missive: messengers. Particularly at this period in the **P. 47 L. 14**
development of his style Shakespeare often uses the
abstract word for the concrete.

Or if you borrow ... : Enobarbus breaks into this **P. 48 L. 14**
emotional conversation with cynical prose, express-
ing his crude commonsense.

presence: noble company. In Court the Presence, or **P. 48 L. 21**
Presence Chamber, was the room where the King
appeared in state.

your considerate stone: 'I will be as dumb as a stone, **P. 48 L. 23**
but I shall think all the same.'

Truths would be ... truths: 'if Antony is united to **P. 49 L. 14**
Octavius through his love of Octavia, even true
causes of quarrel would be regarded as idle tales,
where now false tales pass for truth.'

P. 49 L. 18   *studied not a present thought:* well considered, not a sudden plan.

P. 50 L. 26   *my sister's view:* to visit my sister.

P. 51 L. 5   *stay'd well by 't:* had a good time.

P. 51 L. 6   *sleep day out of countenance:* flouted day by keeping awake only at night.

P. 51 L. 10   *fly by an eagle:* a fly compared with an eagle.

P. 51 L. 20   *The barge she sat in:* For Plutarch's account of this first meeting see Introduction p. 16. It is superb artistry to give this lyrical and rapturous account of Cleopatra to Enobarbus, who is usually so laconic and cynical.

P. 51 L. 31   *fancy out-work Nature:* imagination create more than natural beauty.

P. 52 L. 2   *what they undid did:* although cooling yet the cheeks grew warm.

P. 52 L. 4   *Nereides:* daughters of Nereus, sea nymphs.

P. 52 L. 5   *tended her ... adornings:* A difficult phrase, much disputed. It means 'they watched her slightest glance as they bowed prettily to fulfil her pleasure.' This is another instance of Shakespeare's overflowing style: he short-circuits grammar.

P. 52 L. 9   *yarely frame the office:* carry out the task like good sailors. *Yarely:* workmanlike.

P. 52 L. 14   *but for vacancy:* but that it caused a vacuum.

P. 53 L. 24   *kept my square:* 'kept straight.'

P. 54 L. 4   *in my motion:* intuitively.

P. 56 L. 24   *sword Philippan:* the sword that Antony wore at his victory at Philippi.

P. 57 L. 11   *tart a favour:* sour a face.

P. 57 L. 28   *it does allay:* mix something base with the previous good news.

P. 59 L. 25   *Narcissus:* a youth so beautiful that he fell in love with his own reflection in the water and perished seeking it.

That art not … sure of: you are not a knave though P. 59 L. 33
your true news is knavish.

ghosted: haunted. The episode is in *Julius Cæsar*, P. 61 L. 8
Act IV, Scene 2.

one man but a man: i.e. and not a king. P. 61 L. 14

from the present: beside the point. P. 61 L. 28

he will to his Egyptian dish again: As always, Enobar- P. 65 L. 9
bus knows his Antony.

He married but his occasion here: i.e. to suit his imme- P. 65 L. 13
diate need.

almsdrink: portions left over and given to the poor. P. 65 L. 28

partisan: a spear, with a long blade with projecting P. 66 L. 5
points – a heavy weapon.

To be call'd … cheeks: A complex image: it may be P. 66 L. 6
paraphrased 'To be summoned to great place, like a
planet in the sky, and then to be a failure is to be
like eyeless sockets which pitifully scar the face.'

I'll ne'er out: I won't miss my turn. P. 66 L. 26

elements: 'Element' is used loosely for any quality. P. 67 L. 10
In Shakespeare's time (and to-day in academic liter-
ary jargon), as Feste remarks, 'the word is over-
worn.' Antony means 'life'.

held my cap off: been the servant to. Servants acknow- P. 67 L. 23
ledged their inferiority by standing bare-headed
before their masters.

you sink: Here Lepidus sinks into coma. P. 67 L. 27

strike the vessels hoa: A disputed phrase, meaning P. 69 L. 6
either 'tap fresh casks' *or* 'bang the cans and make a
noise.'

Lethe: the River of Forgetfulness in the Under- P. 69 L. 19
world.

darting Parthia: The Parthians were usually able to P. 70 L. 28
harass the heavy-armed Roman armies by their
method of riding up close to the legionaries, flinging
their darts and retreating quickly. Marcus Crassus,
the third member of the first triumvirate (with Julius

Cæsar and Pompey) was defeated and killed by the Parthians under Pacorus' father, Orodes.

P. 71 L. 11   *A lower place … great an act:* i.e. subordinates must not distinguish themselves too greatly.

P. 72 L. 16   *green sickness:* a form of anaemia common in girls.

P. 72 L. 18   *oh how he loves Cæsar:* Here they mimic Lepidus' complimentary manners.

P. 72 L. 23   *Arabian bird:* the phoenix of legend. Only one phoenix lived at any time.

P. 73 L. 4   *shards:* the hard wings of the beetle.

P. 73 L. 11   *farthest band … approof:* as my most extravagant guarantee shall be honoured.

P. 74 L. 5   *The swans' down feather:* Octavia is so overcome by her emotion that she cannot speak or be silent.

P. 74 L. 9   *cloud in's face … horse:* a cloud is a dark patch between a horse's eyes, denoting bad temper.

P. 75 L. 7   *Herod of Jewry:* See note p. 26, l. 14.

P. 75 L. 29   *She creeps … breather:* Octavia is demure and insignificant; moving or standing she is statuesque.

P. 76 L. 17   *forehead As low:* A low forehead was regarded as ugly, and the sign of stupidity. Cleopatra is now satisfied; her rival, after all, is a dull, unintelligent, round-faced little widow.

P. 77 L. 17   *from his teeth:* 'his praises were from the lips, not the heart.'

P. 78 L. 2   *branchless:* bare of honour.

P. 79 L. 18   *Contemning Rome:* There was no hint of Antony's return to Cleopatra when he parted from Octavia: but the moment she has gone, all restraint is thrown off and he returns to his old mistress. Cæsar's sudden burst of indignation is a very effective way of showing the quick change.

P. 79 L. 23   *Cæsarion:* Cleopatra's son by Julius Cæsar.

P. 80 L. 33   *The wife of Antony:* i.e. my sister and Antony's wife should travel like a Queen, royally escorted.

ostentation of our love: public show of my love.   P. 81 L. 9

But let determin'd things ... their way: Cæsar, as the   P. 82 L. 14
soothsayer has already observed, is Destiny's darling.

gives his potent regiment ... noises it against us: has   P. 82 L. 26
surrendered his powerful authority to a whore who
clamours against us.

But why, why, why?: Enobarbus shows no respect   P. 83 L. 4
for Cleopatra, whom he regards familiarly as Antony's mistress.

If not, denounc'd: 'the war has been declared against   P. 83 L. 8
me, why should I therefore not be present?'

Ingross'd by swift impress: hurriedly conscripted.   P. 84 L. 16

Thetis: a sea nymph.   P. 85 L. 11

III. 8: In the accepted text the play is divided into   P. 86
a number of little scenes, each with its own locality.
Shakespeare, however, is here following a technique
much used in the cinema: he gives a number of brief
glimpses of the various characters to show how the
swift progress of events is affecting each.

token'd pestilence, Where death is sure: like the plague   P. 87 L. 19
when the spots denoting death appear. Shakespeare's
audience were unpleasantly familiar with the plague:
there had been a violent outbreak in 1603 in London
which carried off more than 25,000 persons.

vantage like a pair of twins ... elder: Scaurus in his   P. 87 L. 22
indignation is not entirely coherent: he means 'vic-
tory seemed to favour both sides, on the whole ours
rather than theirs.'

(The breese upon her) ... flies: 'like a cow, stung by   P. 87 L. 24
a gadfly, racing about a field with her tail stuck out.'

loof'd: luffed, i.e. having turned her head toward the   P. 87 L. 29
wind to make off.

doting mallard: a wild drake, flying after the duck.   P. 87 L. 31

lated in the world: like one who has stayed out too   P. 88 L. 27
late and lost his way in the dark.

show their shoulders: turn their backs to the enemy.   P. 89 L. 2

P. 89 L. 17   *lost command:* both of tongue and self.

P. 89 L. 31ff   *he at Philippi ... yet now:* Antony, oblivious to all around him, is brooding on the contrast between the present and the past, when he and Cæsar commanded together at Philippi. *Like a dancer:* i.e. with sword sheathed. *Dealt on lieutenantry:* let his subordinates do the fighting. *Squares:* squadrons.

P. 90 L. 7   *unqualitied:* unmanned: lost his proper quality.

P. 90 L. 8   *sustain me:* Cleopatra once more draws attention to herself by swooning.

P. 91 L. 14   *Enter ... Thidias:* Shakespeare called his character Thidias. Editors (knowing better) correct the name to Thyreus.

P. 91 L. 26   *I was of late ... grand sea:* 'I am as insignificant compared with Antony, as a dewdrop to the Ocean.'

P. 92 L. 26   *how Antony: becomes his flaw:* how he behaves now he is a broken man.

P. 93 L. 4   *Think, and die:* 'Don't talk: die in silence.'

P. 93 L. 13   *meered question:* the sole matter in dispute. .

P. 94 L. 2   *To lay his gay comparisons apart ... declin'd:* to lay aside his gay signs that he is a young man, and now superior, and meet me in my decline.

P. 94 L. 6   *high-battl'd:* with great armies.

P. 94 L. 7   *Unstate his happiness:* disregard his superiority.

P. 94 L. 7   *be stag'd to th' show:* like an amateur competing on the stage against a professional fencer. Such combats were common in Elizabethan theatres.

P. 94 L. 8   *judgements are ... fortunes:* when a man's luck turns he loses his sense.

P. 94 L. 12   *Knowing all measures:* having experience of all kinds of fortune.

P. 95 L. 14   *He is a God:* Cleopatra begins to show herself the essential harlot, as she turns to a new and better customer.

P. 95 L. 33   *in deputation:* as my representative.

Wisdom ... shake it: 'if you do the wise thing no ill luck will follow.'   P. 96 L. 6

Since she was Cleopatra: since she has forgotten that she is a Queen.   P. 97 L. 2

God quit you: God requite you – 'thank you kindly, sir.'   P. 97 L. 32

hill of Basan ... horned herd: A reminiscence of two lines in the *Psalms* (68 v. 15 and 22 v. 12); 'as the hill of Basan, so is God's hill: even an high hill as the hill of Basan' and 'fat bulls of Basan close me in on every side.'   P. 98 L. 2

terrene Moon: earthly moon, i.e. Cleopatra.   P. 98 L. 32

ties his points: the hose (breeches) in Shakespeare's time were kept up by being fastened to the doublet with points or laces. It was the business of the servant to fasten them.   P. 99 L. 3

our Chronicle: our place in history.   P. 99 L. 24

I will seek Some way to leave him: Even Enobarbus deserts: he can follow a defeated master but not a madman.   P. 100 L. 21

calls me Boy: a gross and intentional insult.   P. 100 L. 27

Enough to fetch him in: i.e. to take him, like a solitary outlaw.   P. 101 L. 12

Take all: i.e. no surrender.   P. 101 L. 29

the witch take me: may I be bewitched.   P. 103 L. 4

quarter: the limit of our guard.   P. 104 L. 18

royal occupation: work for kings, i.e. war.   P. 105 L. 16

Riveted trim: 'riveted finery'. i.e. armour.   P. 105 L. 24

soldier's kiss ... mechanic compliment: i.e. a curt kiss is the soldier's farewell, a civilian is more demonstrative in his farewells. *Mechanic:* belonging to a working man.   P. 106 L. 2

Go Eros ... : This is the divine spark in Antony which cheats such as Octavius of their victory.   P. 107 L. 2

subscribe: sign.   P. 107 L. 4

P. 109 L. 5   *our oppression:* the strength opposed to us.

P. 109 L. 16   *H:* with a pun on *ache* which was pronounced as 'H'.

P. 109 L. 19   *scotches:* gashes, i.e. there is still room for a few more wounds in my body.

P. 110 L. 9   *as you serv'd the cause:* not as followers but as principals.

P. 110 L. 18   *thou day o' th' world:* 'brightest of all creatures'.

P. 110 L. 20   *proof of harness:* armour of proof.

P. 110. L. 26   *world's great snare:* i.e. the uncertainty of war.

P. 111 L. 22   *court of guard:* the headquarters of the guard.

P. 112 L. 4   *Oh sovereign Mistress of true melancholy:* the Moon, mistress of the Night, which is the time for the most melancholy brooding.

P. 112 L. 12   *thine own particular:* so far as you yourself are concerned.

P. 114 L. 13   *Triple-turn'd whore:* 'one who has double-crossed three men.'

P. 114 L. 22   *spaniel'd:* for the Folio reading 'pannelled.'

P. 114 L. 30   *heart of loss:* centre, i.e. utter loss.

P. 115 L. 6   *Most monster-like:* i.e. like a freak in a fair.

P. 115 L. 15   *shirt of Nessus:* The centaur Nessus when fatally wounded by Hercules told Deianira (his bride) to give him a shirt dipped in the blood. The shirt was brought to Hercules by Lichas, but when he put it on, it stuck to his flesh and began to consume him. In his agony Hercules threw Lichas into the sea and then slew himself. *Alcides:* Hercules.

P. 115 L. 26   *Telamon:* Ajax, who went mad with disappointment when Achilles' shield was awarded to Ulysses and not to himself.

P. 116 L. 11   *Sometime we see … dragonish:* a cloud shaped like a snake. The contrast in tone here is notable. The fury of Antony's last speech has diminished into a quiet pathos.

black Vesper's pageants: things seen in the evening. P. 116 L. 18

rack dislimns: the drifting cloud paints out. P. 116 L. 21

Pack'd cards: cheated in the deal. P. 116 L. 31

The seven-fold shield ... heart: Even Achilles' shield P.117 L. 26
with its seven layers of hide cannot ward off troubles
which assault the heart.

seal then: finish, the act of sealing being the com- P.118 L. 5
pleting of a legal agreement.

enter me: enter me in his good books. P. 120 L. 20

our size of sorrow: our sorrow must be equal to our P. 122 L. 2
cause.

Demuring upon me: looking down at me primly. P. 123 L. 2

pole: Pole-star, guiding star. P. 124 L. 13

chares: household tasks, performed by a charwoman. P. 124 L. 27

He mocks ... makes: his delays are a mockery. P. 125 L. 17

The round World: at Antony's death there should P. 126 L. 3
have been such portents as before Julius Cæsar died.

single doom: merely the death of one man. P. 126 L. 6

When such a spacious ... himself: in Antony's death P. 126 L. 26
he sees what might have been his fate.

top of all design: supreme conception. P. 127 L. 3

quality of her passion: nature of her sorrow. P. 127 L. 28

Fortune's knave: servant to Fortune. P. 128 L. 18

never palates more the dung, The beggar's nurse, and P. 128 L. 22
Cæsar's: This phrase has been much disputed, and
unnecessarily emended. It means: 'Death make us
sleep, and never more eat the dung [i.e. food grown
out of manure], which nourishes alike the beggar and
Cæsar.' It is an echo of Antony's 'our dungy earth
alike feeds beast as man' (p. 24, l 16.). Morbid brood-
ings on the odd transmutation of matter are common
in poetry of the early seventeenth century. Thus
Hamlet traces the noble dust of Alexander till he
finds it stopping a bung hole.

P. 128 L. 24   *Enter Proculeius:* Modern editors rewrite this scene by changing the older stage direction to *Enter, by the gates of the monument, Proculeius, Gallus, and soldiers;* they omit, however, to explain how the action could have been carried out on the Elizabethan stage.

P. 129 L. 3   *care to be:* care whether I am.

P. 129 L. 17   *pray in aid for kindness:* beg to be allowed to be kind to you.

P. 129 L. 28   *You see ...:* In the Folio, there is no stage direction but a second speech heading of *Pro* is added before 'You see'. The soldiers clearly enter at this point.

    Modern editors, remembering Plutarch and forgetting the Elizabethan stage, give this speech to Gallus (who is not introduced into the Scene in the Folio) and add the stage direction:

    Here Proculeius and two of the Guard ascend the monument by a ladder placed against a window and, having ascended, come behind Cleopatra. Some of the Guard unbar and open the gates.

    There is nothing of this in the Folio.

P. 130 L. 21   *shouting valetry:* mob of yelling slaves.

P. 131 L. 26   *propertied:* had the quality of music like the perfect harmony of music of the spheres.

P. 132 L. 10   *vie strange forms with fancy:* to invent such imaginary beings as will vie with Antony.

P. 132 L. 11   *Nature's piece, 'gainst Fancy:* Nature's masterpiece (Antony) was greater than any man that could be imagined.

P. 132 L. 15   *would I ... success:* 'ill luck take me.'

P. 133 L. 26   *scutcheons:* coats of arms displayed at funerals and other ceremonial occasions.

P. 133 L. 31   *Not petty things admitted:* not merely the trifles.

P. 134 L. 24   *Parcel the sum:* add to the sum.

P. 135 L. 12   *roll of conquest:* record of the victory.

P. 135 L. 14   *make prize with you:* reckon the value.

P. 135 L. 25   *words:* tries to win me by words.

the bright day is done And we are for the dark: This P. 135 L. 28
echoes Antony's words (p. 117, l 21) 'Unarm Eros,
the long day's task is done, And we must sleep.'
The play is full of poignant, contrasting echoes. To
Antony, the day's end brings rest after labour; to
Cleopatra darkness after brightness.

Egyptian puppet: a figure in a puppet show. P. 136 L. 20

scald rhymers ... whore: Any sensational event was P. 136 L. 27
at once celebrated in a ballad, usually of execrable
doggerel, and sung to the tune of some popular
song. The players, too, being the 'abstracts and brief
chronicles of the time' enacted history and contem-
porary events as closely as they dared. In 1600, in
the time of his disgrace, Essex moaned 'The prating
tavern haunter speaks of me what he lists: they print
me and make me speak to the world, and shortly
they will play me upon the stage.' In 1608 the company of Children of Blackfriars were disbanded because in spite of formal prohibition they dramatized
recent French history, bringing Henri IV on the
stage, and showing a scene where his Queen and
his mistress came to blows: all were still alive.

boy my greatness: women's parts were acted by boys. P. 136 L. 33

I am again for Cydnus To meet Mark Antony: Another P. 137 L. 12
echo, recalling Enobarbus' magnificent account (p.
51 l. 19). Cleopatra at this supreme moment is once
more in the ecstatic mood of her greatest triumph.

fleeting Moon: because the inconstant moon, ever P. 137 L. 29
changing, has been the appropriate symbol of one
who had so many lovers.

do his kind: act after his kind, according to his nature. P. 138 L. 21

luck ... after wrath: the Gods give men luck which P. 139 L. 14
brings down on them the divine wrath.

ass, unpolicied: cheated in his politic tricks. P. 140 L. 4

Touch their effects: are realized. P. 141 L. 6

GLOSSARY

abstract: summary, epitome
admiral: the admiral's ship
admitted: permitted to enter
angle: fishing rod
answer: made answerable for
antick'd: made fools of
appeal: impeachment
approves: corroborates
arrant: errand
aspic: asp
atone: make one, unite

band: bond
banquet: wine and light refreshments
bark'd: stripped bare
bench-holes: privies.
blown: swollen
blows: makes to swell
boggler: shifty thing
boot: advantage
bourn: boundary, limit
brave: insult
brief: summary
broached: opened (like a cask)
brooch'd: adorned
burgonet: helmet, and so protector

cantle: segment
carbuncled: jewelled
chance: misfortune
change: i.e. of Fortune
chap: cheek, jaw
charm: that which bewitches
chuck: chick, dear

cinders: hot embers
circle: the crown
clip: embrace
clouts: rags, bandages
cloyless: which never jades the taste
colour: excuse
compare: agree
competitor: partner
composure: composition
conditions: dispositions
confound: waste
constrained: forced
contemning: despising
continent: that which contains
corrigible: submissive
counts: reckonings
curious: precise

daff: doff, put off
demon: guardian spirit
demurely: with subdued sound
determines: comes to an end
diminutives: poor creature
discandying: melting
discredit: make discreditable
disponge: squeeze out, drop
dissuade: draw to change his inclination
distractions: small parties

ear: plough
elements: sky, weather
embossed: foaming at the mouth, hard driven
enfranchis'd: liberated

ensued: followed
estridge: hawk
exigent: emergency
expedience: haste
eyne: eyes

factors: agents
fairy: enchantress
fats: vats
fear: frighten.
feeders: servants
fleet: float
flush: lusty, full of energy
foison: plenty
formal: of normal shape
forspoke: spoken against
fretted: frayed
frustrate: frustrated, thwarted
furious: mad

garboils: tumults, commotions
gests: brave deeds
grates: irritates

halt: limping
hazarded: forfeited
high-battl'd: with great armies
holding: burden, chorus
homager: vassal

immoment: slight
import: involve
inhoop'd: confined in the ring
intrinsicate: intricate.

Jack: knave

kite: feeder on offal

lank'd: grew lean
launch: lance

length: prolonging of life
levell'd: aimed, guessed
lottery: prize
luxuriously: lustfully

mark: range
mirth: joke
modern: new, and so not great-
　　ly valued.
moe: more
moiety: part
muss: scramble

nick'd: snipped, cut short
non-pareil: unequalled

odds: superiority
o'ercount: cheat
ordinary: dinner
owe: own

pales: fences in
pall'd: decayed
passion: emotion
period: full stop, end
plated: armed
plates: coins
pleach'd: folded
port: (1) gate, (2) noble bearing
possess it: have your wish
practise: plot
pregnant: probable
presently: immediately
prevented: forestalled
project: set forth
purge: seek a drastic remedy
pursed: put in the purse

quit: requite, pay back

ranges: ranks
rated: apportioned
rates: is worth
raught: snatched away
rheum: a running at the eyes
ribaudred: foul
riggish: naughty, wanton
rivality: partnership
rive: split.

safed: safeguarded
salt: sensual
scald: scurvy
seel: make blind the eyes of a hawk by tying the eyelids.
semblable: like
shroud: protecting cover
signs well: is a good sign
soils: blemishes
sovereign: potent
square: (1) quarrel, (2) accurately measure.
spaniell'd: followed like a dog
stain: discredit
still: always
stomach: (1) be angry, (2) inclination
synod: assembly

tabourines: drums
tall: brave
targes: targets, small shields
tawny front: dusky brow
three-nook'd: three-cornered
touches: affects closely
traduc'd: condemned
tribunal: judgment seat
troops: followers

unfolded: exposed
unseminar'd: gelded

vacancy: leisure
vant: vanguard
vented: uttered

waned: failing
weet: know
will: inclination, lust
window'd: standing at a window
worm: snake
wrinkled deep: growing old

yare: neatly handled, workmanlike